Feeling her heat as I ran my hands over her body caused my breathing to quicken. I knelt, took her breasts in my hands and, with my tongue, wrote her name in wet letters on the smooth flesh of her stomach.

After a moment, I forgot how to spell *Ellen* so I licked what I could, finally sinking to my heels so that her pubic hair was within reach. I wrapped my arms low around her hips and made a trail down as far as my tongue could reach.

I was digging my way through her silky brush when I became conscious of her movement away from me. "What? What's the matter?"

Time and Time Again

Catherine Ennis

THE NAIAD PRESS, INC.
1996

Printed in the United States of America on acid-free paper
First Edition

Editor: Lisa Epson
Cover designer: Bonnie Liss (Phoenix Graphics)
Typesetter: Sandi Stancil

Library of Congress Cataloging-in-Publication Data

Ennis, Catherine, 1937 –
    Time and time again / by Catherine Ennis.
        p.   cm.
    ISBN 1-56280-145-7 (pbk.)
    1. Lesbians—Fiction. I. Title.
PS3555.N6T5   1996
813'.54—dc20

96-26683
CIP

About the Author

Catherine Ennis enjoys writing about things that give her pleasure. Her novels reflect the environment and culture of the area in which she has spent most of her adult years — New Orleans, and southern Louisiana in general.

The diversity of her characters matches the diversity of her many friends, who encourage as well as inspire her writing.

Catherine's interests and tastes are eclectic, but paramount among them is a fondness for oral gratification; she likes to grow food, cook food, and above all, eat food.

For authenticity, Catherine revisited her favorite places in the French Quarter in order to recapture the ambiance of this special place, the locale of this, her sixth book.

Chapter 1

Morning is brighter on the coast. Even with blinds and drapes closed, the bedroom seems flooded with light when the sun barely begins to peek over the Gulf's gray water. The windows face east so the light isn't a big surprise, but it's a decided inconvenience if we'd planned to sleep late.

Eyes closed, I rolled over and reached for Ellen. My hand touched pillow and rumpled bedclothes but not her soft body. I squinted at the place where she should have been.

"Honey, where are you?" Thinking she was in the

1

bathroom, I hardly raised my voice. She didn't answer.

I tried a little louder, "Ellen, where are you?"

I heard little clinking sounds coming from the back of the house. Grumbling, I grabbed my robe and stalked into the kitchen. Ellen was stirring something in a bowl, and the table, set for four, had a vase of yellow driveway weeds in the center.

She looked up, smiling her welcome. "I know we're completely alone and, personally, I like you naked, but Lou and Peaches will be here for the weekend any time now. For breakfast, too, remember?" She looked at my feet. "You might also try wearing shoes."

"I don't need shoes," I said petulantly. "I'm naked because I wanted to make love. It's Saturday morning and that's what I planned." I slipped my arms into the robe, pulling it loosely around me.

"Well, maybe there's time . . ." Ellen's voice trailed into silence. We both heard the sound of tires on my newly graveled drive.

"No," she said after a moment, with a tiny shrug. "No, I don't think so."

I was peeved. "Why didn't you wake me?"

"You were sleeping like a log. I didn't have the heart."

We heard Lou's rumbling laughter and the sound of footsteps on the tiny landing. Clutching my robe around me, I stalked back into the bedroom. "You should have asked them to get here for lunch instead," I muttered under my breath.

It had been this way for a while. Ellen just was not interested in making love. Lately I had been the one to initiate lovemaking and, although Ellen usually

2

responded, I sensed a lack of enthusiasm. She made the right moves, but I often got the feeling that she'd rather be doing something else.

My two-minute shower over, I dried and dressed in shorts and a sleeveless top. Shoes could wait. They'd all seen my bare feet.

The kitchen smelled of biscuits and bacon, and Peaches and Ellen were watching something sizzle in a frying pan. I pulled out a chair across from Lou. "How ya doin', Lou?" I asked, propping elbows on the table.

"Okay, Millie," she answered. Then, leaning toward me, her voice now a whisper, "I'm thinking of buying a place over here. I've always liked the coast, you know." She was nodding, eyebrows slightly raised.

I smiled, not at all surprised. Mississippi has many miles of coastline with clean sand beaches that glitter white in the sunshine. Until a killer hurricane struck, everybody had liked this stretch of coast, but people hadn't flocked back to rebuild. A big reason was probably that the beach and the beach road no longer existed. At high tide the water lapped where the roads had been.

Of course, there wasn't much of anything left where Gertrude had come ashore. Farther east and west of here things were blown around, but there was nothing like the devastation of her direct hit. Gertrude had perched offshore for two days and in that time had completely eroded the beach and destroyed everything her winds had touched. Then she made an unexpected reversal of direction and lumbered back into the Gulf of Mexico, only to hit Florida and points north. Here, even though her winds had gone inland for only a few miles, she'd left a clean sweep before changing course.

For safety from an ordinary storm surge, my cottage was built on tall, creosoted pilings to allow gulf water to wash under. It had been a weekend spot for us since Lou's father helped me build it soon after the most destructive hurricane in the history of the coast.

That hurricane, the seventh of the season, was the reason I was so broke. All of the homes in the area fronting the beach had been swept away, leaving not a trace. The people who had owned my lot, after surveying the devastation, sold me the tree stumps, shattered concrete walkways, and sinkholes filled with dead fish for much less than waterfront property is worth. I knew next year's storm could blow it all away again but, after much soul searching, I decided to borrow the money and take my chances. Buying the small lot next to mine meant I could add a garage some day, if I ever bought a car.

"Do you have anyplace in mind, Lou?" I lowered my voice conspiratorially. "Does Peaches know about this?" I asked.

Lou glanced over her shoulder. "No, it's a surprise. But I've already picked out a place. Remember that antebellum mansion north of here, a place called The Oaks, where there's still part of a chimney standing? Like everything else on this stretch of beach, it's for sale."

Yes, I knew it well. It was one of the first homes, and certainly the largest on the coast. Its ancient brick construction had withstood dozens of hurricanes for over a century and a half. It had been opened to the public several years ago, and I had toured the

4

interior and walked the lovely formal gardens more than once.

"They'll want an arm and a leg," I said.

"Actually they don't. There's nothing left except that broken chimney, part of a concrete walkway, and some crumbled steps near the road. Every single brick in the house was blown into the next county, so what's there to sell?" Lou was frowning. "Nobody wants to rebuild on this stretch of coast; they're all still too scared, except you and me and maybe a few other crazies."

I had to smile. "So," I said, "we're crazy."

Lou shrugged. "Well, yeah. But you've always known that, haven't you?"

My smile broadened as I remembered Lou and our high school days. "Yeah, that's no secret for sure."

"After we eat, let's drive up the coast." Lou's voice was still hushed. "Peaches doesn't have to know why we're looking, but I want to explore the property, get a feel for it, okay?" There was an expression on her craggy face that I hadn't seen before, a heavy sadness not concealed by the normalcy of her tone. I nodded, wondering if what I considered my growing problem with Ellen was making my imagination work overtime.

A drive was okay with all of us, so after breakfast we piled into Lou's Lincoln and headed north. I was still kind of pissed, knowing that having Lou and Peaches in the next room effectively canceled any thoughts of having sex that night.

Ellen's climax is hardly more than a gentle shudder, a quiet sigh. On the other hand, I heave and groan, with motion and sound escalating as orgasm nears. I finally explode with enough noise to wake the dead. On a quiet night, even with the door shut, I could be heard with a pillow over my head.

Before Gertrude there had been parallel roads skirting the water. One was on a natural rise of several feet for traffic going west toward Louisiana. The other was built on crystal white sand carted in by the truckload and dumped on top of the original beach sand. The road we were on, with its concrete seawall, carried traffic east toward Alabama. Gertrude's one-hundred-and-eighty-mile winds had picked up the concrete from most of both roads, depositing the chunks who knows where and leaving only bits and pieces sticking up out of the sand. At high tide, shallow water now sloshed where the roads had been.

Of necessity, Lou drove east on what remained of the west road, detouring potholes, sandpiles, and blank places where it had risen up and flown away. A few cars were parked here and there, and a handful of people were walking around on what was left of a coastline swept barren by wind and water.

For the first time, I also saw construction — not brick mansions, but creosoted pilings that reached far above the ground. Like my cottage, these places seemed to be small wooden structures for weekend pleasure, places we natives call a camp.

"They're looking for treasure?" Peaches asked, seeing metal detectors.

"Who knows what they're doing? They may just be gawkers. Or maybe they owned a place and are looking for what's left. There aren't any landmarks anymore, that's for sure." Lou slowed to a crawl, carefully crossing a section where there wasn't any road, just fine sand that caught at the big car and made it slip sideways.

"Maybe we ought to go back," Peaches said nervously, her eyes on a finger of gray water that had puddled across the sand and was almost touching our tires.

"We're okay, hon," Lou assured her, but slowing noticeably.

"Shouldn't there have been barricades or something?" Ellen's voice was anxious. "This isn't a road anymore; it's hardly a path, Lou."

"There were barricades, Ellen, but I went around them. Y'all were too busy talking."

Peaches' voice was louder, "I want to go back before we get stuck in the sand. Lou, turn around."

Lou sighed, shrugging her shoulders. "Okay, but I can't turn here without pontoons. We have to go on to the end where there's still some road to turn around on."

I knew the property she had in mind had been located just around the road's longest curve. We could probably spot it by the chimney, which was the only thing left standing on this stretch of coast where Gertrude had touched first. To our right, the almost glassy stillness of the Gulf mirrored a few gray clouds and patches of blue sky. When the tide came in, it would narrow what was left of the beach, allowing tiny, tentative ripples to create a shoreline where the roads had been.

We rounded the curve and felt our wheels catch on concrete. "Look." Lou pointed to her left at a brick chimney standing tall and alone on the barren ground. "I'd like to see what's left up there where that old place used to be. Looks like the house blew away from around the fireplace, doesn't it?"

Peaches grunted. "If you'd been with Lewis and Clark they'd never have made it out of town. There's nothing there to see, Lou. Let's go!"

I thought it was time to intervene. "I'd like to explore, too. That chimney's pretty old. If there're any around, I may pick up a loose brick for a doorstop. Lotta history there."

"Is it okay, hon?" Lou had stopped the car, her hand on the door handle. "We won't be but a minute." She was sure that I'd go with her, leaving Ellen and Peaches in the car.

"I want to go with you." Ellen wasn't one for having her shoes fill with sand; she'd rather pick her way over a New Orleans sidewalk, sidestepping the debris left by thousands of tourists. I was surprised but figured we'd let her in on Lou's decision to buy the land once Peaches wasn't with us.

"I'm not going to stay here by myself." Peaches' lip was poked out, her displeasure obvious.

Ellen gave me a little shrug. "I'll wait with her," she said. "I don't mind."

"We'll hurry," Lou promised. As she turned away I saw that strange expression again. Peaches was pouting, and Lou was trying to hide her misery. What's going on here? A breakup, perhaps?

All of the homes along this area of coast had been built on a slight rise of ground that gradually sloped down toward the water. Most places had needed several steps, then a long concrete walkway to

8

get from the road to the house, but there were no steps here, just loose sand. We sank almost to our ankles climbing from the road to a short piece of walkway that had escaped the storm. Lou didn't have anything to say, so I kept quiet, too.

I followed her lead as she wandered seemingly without direction but gradually getting closer to the chimney, which was intact except for some missing bricks at the very top.

She stopped suddenly and bent, peering intently at the slab of sand-covered concrete under her feet.

"Found something?" I asked, bending to look at whatever it was that she saw. I didn't see anything, but I kept looking.

"This is really funny."

"What's funny?" I still didn't see anything.

"Listen." Lou stomped her heels on the slab. She was wearing cowboy boots, the ones with thick, hard heels, and I listened as she stomped. I didn't hear an answering sound. I said, "You expect the concrete to talk back?"

"No, but it is talking back. It's definitely talking back."

She knelt, and with her hand she cleared some heaped sand off one edge of the slab. Then she stood and stomped some more. I saw the remaining grains disappear as if in an hourglass, falling out of sight until there was no sand, just a thin, straight line where the slab now appeared to rest on a concrete rim. Where had the sand gone?

"Where did the sand go, Lou?"

"I think there's a hollow place under here; it

9

sounded different when I walked on it. I'll bet this slab is covering something." She knelt and pulled at the slab, but it wouldn't budge. More sand disappeared around the edges.

"Covering what?" I'm an artist, that's how I make my living. I can visualize almost anything, then paint what I've imagined. But this slab and the missing sand didn't stir my imagination at all. "Covering what?" I asked again.

Lou stood, brushed her hands. "I don't know, Millie. But it's hollow under that slab. This place was here before the Civil War; maybe it has something to do with that." She brushed the knees of her pants. "Whatever, I'm going to find out."

"How're you going to do that? You don't own this place."

Lou looked at me kind of funny, then shifted her gaze back to the slab. "I think I do, Millie. I already put money down on it. I didn't tell you because I didn't want to say I'd bought it until the deal was settled. Dad and I came over a couple of weeks ago. He said the coast would recover and that buying coast property was a good investment. We didn't do anything but look at it; then he had it surveyed. Didn't you see the markers?"

I looked around and saw what I hadn't noticed before. Tiny flags fluttered here and there around what I supposed was the property's boundary.

Deciding that our longtime friendship allowed me to ask a personal question, I said, "Lou, is there something going on between you and Peaches? I'm getting vibes."

Lou actually blushed. She bent to brush her knees

again, then straightened and looked across the white sand at the car.

"Peaches and I aren't getting along lately. I don't know what to do. She wants something." Lou paused. "Something more."

"More what?" I didn't really want to know, the words just popped out. "Wait!" I touched Lou's arm. "I didn't mean to pry. Don't say a word."

"It's okay, Millie," Lou shrugged. "We'll work it out."

"In that case, what do you plan to do about your hollow whatever-it-is?"

"We're going to a hardware store and get a couple of pry bars. There's something here. You know, maybe pirate treasure."

"Yeah, and maybe a tomb from the Civil War. We might turn out to be grave robbers. Wouldn't Ellen and Peaches love that?"

"Doesn't matter. I've gotta open it." She turned and headed for the car.

Chapter 2

"I need some tools," Lou announced, as she opened the car door.

Peaches' frown was thunderous. "Tools for what, may I ask? You've got enough stuff in the trunk to build a hotel."

Lou's mouth tightened into a grim line. She was in charge of her father's construction firm, supervising work crews and inspecting jobs in progress during the week.

After the carpenters had finished the framing, the roof, and the siding on my cottage, Lou had taken over. She had worked every weekend on the inside, hauling tools back and forth from the city. She supervised the plumbing and installed the inside wiring and walls. Ellen and I worked as her apprentices, but, without Lou to show us the way, we wouldn't have been past home plate. No wonder the car's trunk was loaded with tools.

"I don't have what I want," Lou said flatly. Ignoring Peaches, she turned to Ellen. "It'll only take a little while. We'll go to the nearest hardware store; I'll get what I need, then I'll treat y'all to something cold. How's that?"

I took Ellen's hand in mine, squeezing. Ellen looked at Lou for a second then, smiling, said, "That's great, Lou." I squeezed again.

Peaches didn't say anything during the rest of the ride. Lou had to drive several miles inland before she found a store that was still in one piece and had stuff to sell. It was already sold out of most things because the people living nearby still had structures in need of repair. Buildings were standing, yes, but missing necessary parts. I heard the sound of hammering from all directions. Lou finally located pry bars in a feed and seed store that featured tiny yellow chicks for sale.

As Lou and I walked out of the store I pointed across the street. "There's a café. It looks decent. Y'all want to try it?"

Lou hefted the four-foot pry bars. "Okay, Millie, but let's see what the girls say."

My Ellen smiled at me. "Okay," she said agreeably, opening her door. Peaches didn't answer even though I was the one to ask the question. Lou stared at her before turning away with a grunt. The

13

three of us walked to the café, leaving Peaches in the car. We each had a Coke, but it wasn't the most fun-filled party I've ever attended.

Back at the car we found Peaches in tears. Lou started the engine, saying, "Well, I asked! You didn't have to sit here alone! It was your idea, remember?" Her voice was cold. Neither of them talked on the way back. I kept Ellen's soft hand in mine, our arms and shoulders touching.

By the time we reached Lou's property, the frigid silence from the front seat was giving me the shivers. It was a relief to walk on the warm sand again. Lou headed directly for the concrete slab. Ellen and I followed closely.

Lou shoved the flat end of one bar into a tiny crack between the slab and the concrete it sat on; then she pushed down hard on the free end. I could hear a grating sound, and the slab moved about a sixteenth of an inch.

"Millie, jam that other bar here next to mine."

I did. Lou and I both pushed down on the free end of my bar, and the slab lifted half an inch. That's how we finally raised it enough to slide it aside, one inch at a time.

"There's a hole under here! I told you there was!" Lou was excited. She knelt on the edge of the opening we had uncovered. It was slightly smaller than the slab. Ellen and I knelt and peered down into darkness. The sun, almost directly overhead, lit only enough for us to see our reflections in water at the bottom of the hole. There was no way I could guess the size, but even leaning as far as I could, I couldn't see walls. I saw only what looked like crates on four sides. Crates were piled almost up to the opening.

"Millie, hang on to my belt! I'm going to see what's there." Lou lay on her stomach and leaned down into the opening with me hanging on to her belt. Lou is built big and square. It wasn't easy to hold her weight as she dangled over the hole. She kept squirming until most of her body disappeared, with only her legs and rear end visible.

"It's a room, Millie." Her voice sounded hollow, like an echo in a bottle. "It's concrete block, and it's full of crates. The water's only about a foot deep, from what I can tell hanging upside down." She squirmed, trying to lean farther.

I noticed Ellen had both hands clinging to Lou's belt, too. With both of us pulling, we dragged Lou's upper half out of the opening.

"Wait," Lou yelled. "Wait!"

"No, if you want to know what's down there, get a ladder, Lou. You're too heavy for us to dangle in midair." Ellen still had a handful of belt. She shook it for emphasis.

Lou wiggled herself upright. Standing, her shirt and pants gleaming with white sand crystals, she said, "I'd jump down, but there's no way to climb out. Guess I will have to get a ladder." She wasn't too happy about a delay.

"Millie has one of those extension things at her place," Ellen offered. "Let's go get it."

Lou brushed casually at the sand on her clothes. She was already heading for the car. Peaches was standing by the driver's door. "What in heaven's name were you doing squirming in the dirt, Lou?"

She was still upset. Her face was splotchy, but curiosity had won out over anger.

"We found a hole, Peaches. Nothing to interest you."

Peaches snorted. "You're right. There's not much around here to interest me. This place, and you, are boring me out of my mind. I want to go back to New Orleans."

She didn't say she wanted to go home. She wanted to get to New Orleans. Did that mean that where she and Lou lived wasn't a home to her anymore? Maybe I was reading more into it than there was.

We had another silent ride, dodging potholes and slipping over sand. I was busy looking at the signs of new construction here and there. Ellen was silent, too, but what was there to say? I put my hand on her thigh, and she covered my hand with hers. From the looks of it, I supposed Lou and Peaches wouldn't be staying over. I began to have happy thoughts about the night.

The ride to my place and the ride back didn't take over forty minutes. We got my twelve-foot ladder, which proved to be just long enough. Peaches followed us up the rise and minced her way to the opening. She still wasn't talking, but we hardly noticed.

Lou slid the ladder in the hole and scrambled down almost before the ladder splashed bottom. I followed cautiously.

Lou edged one foot into the water, feeling for bottom. Then she stepped the other foot off the rung and looked up at me. The water was about halfway up her boots. I moved to the bottom rung and, wide-eyed, peered around. No, I could see it wasn't a hole in the ground. It was a hole, but a carefully constructed man-made hole. It was a room. It was probably twelve feet by twelve feet, lined with blocks, and the only opening was the one through the ceiling where we'd entered.

Crates, double stacked, lined the walls up to eight feet or so. We could see they held bottles. A couple of the bottom crates had rotted apart in the water, and bottles — some brown, some clear, and a few green — had spilled out. Lou reached and lifted one bottle that was filled with a clear liquid. She uncorked it, put it to her nose and smelled, letting out a whoosh of air.

"This'd set you on your ear, Millie. I don't see labels or tax stamps on any of these bottles, so it's probably homemade stuff. My dad told me about bathtub gin during prohibition. I think that's what this is." She inhaled again, making a face. I half-expected her to take a sip.

I reached for the bottle. One sniff convinced me that Lou was probably right. I'm no connoisseur, being mostly a nondrinker, but if all the crates held bottles, and all the bottles held gin, we were standing in the middle of enough booze to float a battleship. I couldn't assess quality, but the quantity was there for the counting.

"What's down there?" It was Ellen, leaning over the opening, her hand firmly grasping the ladder, trying to look down past my head and shoulders.

"I'm coming up," I told her, "You take my place." I knew Ellen was excited, too. I climbed my way out, squeezing past her. Ellen, clutching the ladder's sides, carefully climbed down. Lou began talking. She was

17

hardly pausing long enough to take a breath, very out of character for her. Then Lou must have upended a bottle. I heard liquid splashing, so I yelled, "Hey, save some for me!"

"Save what?" Peaches was poking me on the shoulder. "What's down there?"

Peaches wasn't talking to Lou, but I wasn't on her list yet, so I answered, "It's a room full of booze. There must be a thousand bottles."

"What kind of booze?"

"The bottles don't have labels. No telling what, but Lou called it bathtub gin."

"Like what bootleggers made? Rumrunner liquor?" Everybody had heard about the rumrunners along the coast during prohibition, the ones who supplied New Orleans, Mobile, and probably every other thirsty place in the coastal south.

"I don't know, Peaches," I answered. "Lou only opened one bottle." Ellen was climbing out; I steadied her and the ladder. "Anything else worth seeing down there?" I asked, holding Ellen's arm just a fraction longer than necessary. She noticed. She looked straight at me with her luminous, brown eyes. Her smile and the slight lift of her eyebrows was clearly an invitation. I smiled back.

This quick exchange wasn't lost on Peaches. Feeling ignored, she spoke louder than necessary. "If that's all there is, think we can go now?"

"Hold your horses," Lou yelled up from the hole. "We're not going anyplace till I'm finished looking around." Hearing this, Peaches started crying again. She turned and ran for the car.

I looked at Ellen, who was slowly shaking her head. She gave a little shrug. "This is all beyond me," she said softly. "What set her off?"

"Damned if I know," I said. "They have problems, I guess."

Ellen likes for things to be on an even keel. She doesn't like fights, isn't sarcastic, and is usually agreeable. Maybe to show that our relationship is on an even keel, she drew a line down my arm, her fingers lightly brushing my breast. It was a very soft touch, but the meaning was obvious.

Ellen isn't flirtatious. She's direct. On our second date Ellen had said, "Let's make love tonight, Millie. We both want to."

I had gulped, said yes, and fallen into bed with her. Ellen was soft and warm and yielding. I wanted her in my arms, between my legs, helping herself to every part of me. I'd had lovers before Ellen, some more knowledgeable, but my satisfaction in awakening Ellen's passion was a pleasure I'd never tired of.

"Tonight?" I asked, wiggling my eyebrows like Groucho.

Ellen smiled, the way she'd smiled that first time. "I think so," she said.

Her words were clues that she understood Lou and Peaches might not be staying the weekend after all.

"I've found something!" Lou's voice held more excitement than a whole roomful of booze had aroused.

I peered past the ladder. Lou was holding up a brown leather suitcase. She climbed without grasping the rungs, handing the case to me before crawling out. "Whatcha think, huh? Do we have a treasure or what?"

I hefted it with one hand, testing. "It's got stuff in it, Lou, but it's not heavy enough to be full of gold."

Lou took it from me. "See," she said, pointing at the locks. "Looks like somebody pried it open." The locks, scratched and bent, were gaping open like they'd been forced, but two leather straps held the case together.

"Open it, Lou." This advice came from Ellen.

"Okay, here goes." Lou put the suitcase on the ground, and the three of us knelt on the sand in front of it, for all the world like supplicants before an altar.

Lou undid the straps and lifted the lid, opening it all the way. I hadn't made any guesses about the contents, and I don't think Ellen had, either. Lou, of course, was kidding about finding a treasure, but I think she expected more than what we saw.

What we saw were clothes. From the flowery pattern of a silky dress packed right on the top, and the lacy underthings neatly folded next to the dress, we knew right away the contents had belonged to a woman. I don't know if Ellen or Lou smelled anything but, as Lou lifted the lid, I caught a whiff of something sweet. It was only for a second or two, just one breath of sweetness before it was gone.

Almost reverently Lou lifted the dress and held it up, being careful not to let it drag in the sand. As if she planned to try it on, she rose from her knees and dangled it in front of her. Lou is a large woman, tall, almost square, heavily muscled with wide

20

shoulders, and the dress, when she held it in front of her, hardly reached her knees. I started to laugh at the absurdity of it, but something stopped me.

The dress was of some thin material, with a small white collar, miniature white buttons, and a pattern of tiny flowers. It could only have been worn by a small person and, from the dress style, that person lived during the twenties or thirties. I did some quick mental calculations. The clothes probably belonged to someone now dead, not a laughing matter.

Ellen lifted a pair of white drawers, holding them for us to see. They were lacy, obviously belonging to a woman, but they looked like boxer shorts — nothing like the briefs we wear today. There was a look of sadness on Ellen's face. She was experiencing the same poignant reaction.

"I feel like I'm desecrating a grave." I looked up at Lou, surprised. She was usually so flat-out unsentimental that her words were unexpected. Lou and Ellen looked at each other, unspeaking. Then, with an abrupt movement, Lou folded the dress and placed it on top of the pile. After a moment, Ellen did the same with the undergarment.

"What's wrong with y'all?" I asked. "It's only an old suitcase full of clothes. Let's see what else is in there."

My words broke the spell. Lou started lifting the top layer and placing everything on the open lid. Two more dresses, more undergarments, a pair of funny-looking shoes with straps on the instep, some lace hankies, and a leather purse with a snap to hold it closed. There was also an envelope with some paper in it.

The little purse held some change and a packet of

neatly folded bills. Almost a thousand dollars in all. Lou grinned from ear to ear. She'd found her treasure.

Ellen was looking into the envelope. She held up a black-and-white snapshot of two young women, arm in arm, smiling into the camera. They were dressed in clothes of the same period as those in the suitcase. She held up a train ticket dated July 24, 1933, for a one-way fare from New Orleans to Chicago. It had not been used. There was also a note that Ellen scanned then read aloud.

Her voice soft, she began, "My darling, you will be with me soon. I am trying to be patient, but my arms ache to hold you. I was never good at waiting, remember? Our apartment is ready, needing only your presence to make it a home. Hurry, dearest. I love you." Ellen looked up. "It's signed 'Helen,'" she said.

Neither Lou nor I spoke. Ellen folded the note and put it back in the envelope. "Whatever her name, she didn't use the ticket, did she?"

My thoughts were bouncing like rubber balls. "This woman, the one who owned the suitcase, was probably going to Chicago to meet Helen." I used the past tense because so many years had gone by since the ticket was issued. I didn't think the ticket's owner was still around to ask for a refund.

Lou closed the lid. "Let's drag that cover back over the opening, Millie. We don't want anyone falling in, do we?"

I had visions of tiny children falling like raindrops into the hole. "I guess not," I answered.

Lou closed the straps and handed the suitcase to Ellen. We dragged the slab back over the opening, and Lou sprinkled sand so that it didn't look like anything was there. Then we walked back to the car. The suitcase dangled from Ellen's hand like what it was, the mildewing relic of a time long past.

Chapter 3

Ellen and I put the suitcase on the seat between us. Although it hadn't been wet, from the years of sitting high and dry on top of some liquor cases it had acquired a mildew odor. Most of the way back to our place I thought about the Helen who had written the note and the woman with the suitcase who was to have met her in Chicago back in 1933.

They sounded like lesbian lovers to me. Did they ever meet, I wondered? Did they finally make a home? Why didn't what's-her-name take her suitcase and money with her on the train to Chicago? I sighed, squeezing Ellen's hand. She squeezed back, effectively erasing Helen and Chicago from my mind. The thought of Ellen naked in our bed and climbing over an equally naked me took over. I grinned at her, marveling again at the instant response I always had when she showed affection. Ellen's wink acknowledged the sexual interplay.

Lou pulled into the newly graveled drive and stopped the car. She turned, her arm across the back of the seat. "I don't think we'll stay; Peaches wants to get to New Orleans. I planned to Sheetrock the kitchen this weekend, but I can do that next time if it's okay with you guys." There were frown lines between her heavy, dark eyebrows.

The cottage was finished on the outside but, except for the large bedroom, the bathroom, and part of the spare bedroom, the inside was a shell. A lot of work was needed to complete the walls, get doors hung, put in molding, finish the wiring, and take care of dozens of other things that Lou would explain when the time came.

With Lou's guidance and Ellen's help, I was doing the taping, sanding, and painting. With what I still owed for the land and what I owed Lou's company for doing the building added to what I'd have to spend on furniture, more gravel for the drive, and various unforeseen expenses, I couldn't afford to hire the job done. Neither Ellen nor I really knew much about finishing work, but we were learning.

"Sure, Lou," I said, opening my door, trying not to seem anxious to get away. "Y'all come by the shop next week. We'll have spaghetti." I had decided to ignore whatever it was that was happening between Lou and Peaches. Over the years I'd watched Lou

25

win, then lose, half a dozen lovers. I had no idea, even now, why Lou's affairs lasted such a short time. I figured it was none of my business. Lou didn't talk, and I didn't ask. Maybe that's what had kept us friends.

"Of course," Ellen was saying, "we could eat something else. Aren't you two tired of spaghetti?" She was opening her door, too. "I'll gladly do the cooking," she added.

I didn't stand around urging them to accept; I wanted to get upstairs.

Lou shrugged. "Keep the suitcase, Ellen. Next time I'm here we'll go through it again. And, if I have a choice, I pick spaghetti." With that, Lou started the engine and backed out of the drive. Neither Ellen nor I had said anything to Peaches, who was ignoring us from the front seat, staring straight ahead, her lips tight.

I carried the suitcase upstairs. Ellen opened the door and, before I could put the suitcase down, turned and put her arms around me, pinning my arms to my sides.

"Let's go to bed now," she said with her usual directness. "We both want to."

"Did you lock the door?"

"What do you think?"

"I think I want to go to bed with you." I dropped the suitcase to the floor.

"Come on, then." She held my hand all the way to the bed.

With Ellen sitting on the bed watching, I undressed first. Then I removed Ellen's clothes. Undressing Ellen is a real turn-on for me. I did it slowly, kissing what I uncovered, caressing her warm

26

flesh, her smooth breasts, lastly helping her to lie back and slowly pulling off her underpants.

I watched her expression as I touched sensitive places, while my hands gently caressed her slim body. Arousal escalated, her brown eyes soon squeezed shut, and her breathing became fast and shallow. With a soft moan she raised her knees, spread her legs, and invited a more intimate touch.

It's really surprising when Ellen is so very ready. She was almost dripping by the time I'd licked my way down to her dark mat of pubic hair. Her hips moved upward, her legs stretched wider to give room to my tongue as I pressed into her warmth.

I wanted to love her slowly, taking my time, but her response made my own excitement grow exponentially. Grasping her tight against me, I let my fingers tease through wetness and circle the tiny mound of flesh that seemed to stretch and harden under my touch. Ellen was breathless, shuddering as I increased both movement and pressure.

Within a minute my fingers were moving inside her, and I moaned encouragingly as I felt her hips jerking. There was no rhythm to our coupling. Ellen's movements were wild, and I clung to her, trying to meet the upward surge of her body.

Her breathing was shallow. With each exhalation I heard a tiny sound; it grew louder until her sudden cry told me that she was coming. I felt the velvet walls in spasm, felt suction as she drew me deep inside, her legs closing to trap my arm.

"Ah, Millie," Ellen whispered, her body slowly relaxing. When she opened her legs, I withdrew my hand.

I leaned on an elbow, looking at her smile. Her

eyes were sleepy. I kissed the faint sheen of perspiration on her forehead. "Oh, Millie," she said softly, pulling my face to hers. Our kiss was deep and satisfying. There was an almost hurtful feeling between my legs when we moved apart.

Ellen turned on her side. "You're next," she said in a whisper, her hand caressing my pubic hair. I seldom needed much foreplay, and her eager response to my lovemaking had made foreplay entirely unnecessary. What I wanted was her touch that very instant.

I guided her hand between my legs and felt her fingers playing in the warm, slippery wetness. My heart started thudding when she began teasing my clit, causing sensation so strong that I cried aloud.

With experience born of many evenings making love on my lumpy mattress, Ellen began dipping into me. She pressed firmly and my flesh stretched, an almost painful but definitely pleasurable feeling. She slid her fingers out, teasing for a moment, then dipped back inside.

I felt spasms between my legs stronger than the tidal wave created when hurricane Gertrude came ashore.

Ellen held me as I tried to get my breathing back to normal. "I'll bet that's what Helen did to her friend," she said softly. "They probably didn't leave their apartment for a week."

"If it was anything like what just happened, they also couldn't walk for a week."

We showered together. Ellen still had sex on her mind. I could tell by the way she soaped my private parts, the way her fingers searched. I almost jumped out of my skin when she hugged my clitoris between

28

thumb and forefinger and began an easy milking motion. I couldn't tell if the liquid running down my inner thighs was mine or the shower spray.

"How's that?" she asked softly. "You like?"

"Yes," I said, widening my knees to give her room. "Ahhh, yes!"

"Do you think Helen and her friend did this when they showered?" Her mouth hard against mine, Ellen was slowly stroking through wetness, circling, entering, then pressing harder with each insertion, causing a momentary loss of speech on my part.

"Uh, yeah," I finally said, my back sliding down the wall as my knees began to give way. Ellen and her busy fingers followed me all the way down.

Dry except for our hair, we cuddled on the bed. I was happier than I'd been in a long time because our lovemaking had been so satisfying ... so wild and deeply satisfying.

I had never seen Ellen so aroused, not even our first time. If this was what happened to her when she fantasized about other lesbians having sex, I'd get a VCR and start renting lesbian movies. "What got you so turned on?" I asked, just to make sure.

"I told you. Thinking about the letter and the apartment in Chicago and the two women who were in love got me to thinking about how it was sixty years ago, what they did. I'll bet they were really in the closet back then." Ellen snuggled her dark head on my shoulder. "Did they make love like us, do you think?"

"Probably. However many ways there are, I guess

they tried. I wonder if they actually ever got together. The train ticket wasn't used, you know."

"Well, that was getaway money in the suitcase. Back then they could have lived for a long time on a thousand dollars. At least, that's what I've heard."

"Get away from what?" I asked, yawning.

"I don't know what, but I think we should try to find out. Don't you?" Ellen sat up. "Honey, I'm hungry. We haven't had any lunch, and my stomach's growling."

"What's in the fridge?" I asked, realizing that I was on the verge of starving. "Stuff for a sandwich, maybe?"

We ate on the tiny balcony, cushioned comfortably in brand-new padded lawn chairs. The Gulf was beginning to kick up. The water wasn't glassy smooth as it had been earlier, and the wind-driven waves were choppy.

"I know it's foolish, but when I feel the wind gusting as hard as it is now it makes me think of Gertrude." Ellen hunched her shoulders, frowning.

"Aw, babe, you don't have to be worried," I said convincingly. "The weather is just what it's always like this time of year. You're supposed to enjoy a gulf breeze, remember?

"Of course. It's just that I remember how bad the hurricane was even in New Orleans, and we only got the tip edge of it. If winds that strong had hit the French Quarter, we'd be dead under a pile of bricks."

She was probably right. The Quarter is one of the oldest places in the South, and much of it is constructed of handmade bricks that date back a couple of hundred years. There are also ancient wooden houses set within touching distance of each other. A really bad blow, or even a major fire, could level what was there in no time. Most of the little shotgun houses had fireplaces that couldn't be used for fear sparks would touch off a blaze.

"What I think is, we should start taping Sheetrock. If we don't get ourselves in gear, there'll never be even one room completely finished."

With a sigh, Ellen rose. She held out her hand. "Come on, then, slave driver."

I followed her into the bedroom. While changing into our grubbies, I watched Ellen slip into her T-shirt. Arms raised high, breasts uncovered, she wiggled the shirt to her shoulders. Before she could grasp the hem to pull it down to her waist, I covered both breasts with my hands, my thumbs caressing her nipples.

She didn't pull away, instead she leaned into me, looked into my eyes, and said, "Food must fuel your sex drive. Are you asking for more?"

I wrapped my arms around her, hugging her warmth against me. "Maybe not this instant, you hussy. The Sheetrock probably can't finish itself, so waiting a few hours will do us good." I kissed the top of her head.

She laughed softly, backed to the bed, and pulled me down on top of her, offering hardened nipples to my mouth.

No way I could refuse the offer. I began sucking her breasts in earnest. I licked the hardened centers, gently scraping with my teeth. My hands claiming her softness, I nursed, making slurping sounds as I squeezed and then blew my warm breath where I had licked.

Ellen's breathing quickened, and she began

31

making little sounds. I felt her hips moving beneath me, rhythmically surging faster as I sucked. Raising my head I asked, "Do you want me to fuck you again?"

"Yes," she hissed, grasping my shoulders. "Yes."

Exhausted, we lay side by side. "Are we going to do this all afternoon, do you think?" Ellen was naked except for the T-shirt, which was bunched around her neck. I had on nothing at all.

"In a way, with all the work we have to do, I hope not. But it's been a long time since we've had sex like this!" Or anything faintly resembling this, I thought. "I've thoroughly enjoyed every minute."

Ellen squeezed my hand. "Me, too," she said.

"In the beginning I couldn't get enough and neither could you. We kind of lost that until today." I paused. "Are you by any chance asking for more?"

Ellen sat up and looked down at me, her eyes bright. "No, I think we should try to do a little Sheetrock instead. I'm not through with you yet, but I can wait until after supper if that's okay with you."

I had to smile. "I'll work with that electric sander if you vacuum the dust, then we can do a little taping. I'd like to try hanging a piece the way I've seen Lou do it. If I get it right, maybe we can have the kitchen walls finished by Sunday evening. Whatcha think?"

Ellen wiggled to the edge of the bed. I ran my

hand down her back. "I'm not trying to start anything, just feeling how smooth you are."

She laughed kind of slow and low. Turning, she looked at me. "I'm going to put flowers on Helen's grave if we ever get to Chicago. I haven't felt this horny since I can't remember when. It's thinking about them making love that's turned me on. But if you've had enough, I guess we can work for a while. We do have all night you know." She arched her eyebrows, grinning.

I lifted my legs to the side of the bed and sat up. "Okay, but keep it in mind, will you?" Unbelievable, but I wanted her again. Probably my libidinous nature trying to make up for the lack of sex recently. Whatever, it had felt great, and waiting for tonight would make it all that much sweeter.

We worked straight through until almost seven o'clock. We put our tools in what was to be the hall closet — when it got walls, that is — and washed for a supper of sandwiches and Cokes. Sitting at the kitchen table talking quietly as the light faded made the little cottage feel like a real home to me.

We were a couple, but we didn't live together. I had my tiny gallery and apartment, if you could call it that, in the New Orleans French Quarter. Ellen lived with her mother in Gentilly, in their family home fronting Lake Pontchartrain.

She had brought her mother to the Quarter one Sunday so that one of the sidewalk artists could do a pastel portrait. Both of them had admired the sample displays I'd hung on the fence behind my easel, so they chose me. Before I'd finished the portrait, I had invited them to visit my studio and gallery on Dumaine Street, one block from Jackson Square.

I really liked Ellen. For six months we were just casual friends. The second time we went out together on what I considered to be a date, we fell into bed. That was shortly before Christmas.

"Ellen, I've wanted to get you in bed for the longest time," I'd whispered that night as we snuggled on my harder-than-hard mattress. It was cold as only New Orleans near the river could be.

"Well, why haven't you told me before, ninny?" Ellen didn't mince words. "I've known you were a lesbian since the day you did Mother's portrait. Why do you think I've been hanging around? Certainly not for your cooking."

Remembering the meal I'd cooked for her in my tiny kitchen, I knew she wasn't kidding. I also knew I'm not gorgeous. I'm tall and thin with plain brown hair and blue eyes, and my hands look like baseball gloves; I can't do much of anything except paint. And I'm shy, painfully shy.

I would have gone on just being a friend if Ellen hadn't practically thrown herself at me. "I thought you were straight," I said to explain my nonaction. "I thought you didn't know about gay people, or that I was one. I don't try to have sex with every woman on two legs as most people think. To be honest," I stuttered, "I didn't think about you that way at all." At least not for the first five minutes, I added silently.

Hearing that, Ellen had moved from my side,

rolled on top of me, and slowly inched her way down my body. I felt her tongue, wet and smooth, tracing a trail down my stomach.

"Do you think about me that way now?" she had asked, running one hand down my front, the other gently pushing my legs apart. I felt her breath on my thighs, her fingers probing, then her tongue, warm and wiggly.

It had been very difficult to concentrate on her words but I tried. "I don't know what I thought at first. I was surprised . . ."

She lifted her head. "Wait," she had said, her voice low and thick. "Just hush now, you can tell me later."

Chapter 4

Halfway back to New Orleans Sunday afternoon we began to argue as I knew we would, even though our weekend had been idyllic and the sex couldn't have been better if I'd planned it. Ellen had responded to my lovemaking with an inventiveness that surprised me. The suitcase, the love letter, and the fact that we were unexpectedly alone must have triggered something, because Ellen had been all over me to my great delight.

We didn't get any Sheetrock hung on Sunday.

What we did was make love, rest from our exertions, eat, then fall on each other again.

I started the argument on our drive back to New Orleans. I knew with my first words that it would have been better to keep my mouth shut. It was the same argument every time we headed home from the coast.

"Ellen," I'd say. "Honey, will you stay with me tonight?" I only asked it because I wanted her to stay with me and not go home to her mother as she always did.

I'd see her shoulders stiffen and her knuckles whiten on the steering wheel. She'd turn her head slowly, as if she had to consider her answer before she faced me.

"No, Millie, I can't do that." Then she'd face the road, increase the speed, and wait for me to have my turn.

"Just this one time?" I knew better than to ask; we'd been through this so often.

"No, Millie, not even this one time."

I honestly couldn't understand why she wouldn't spend the night with me. Sometimes, on a weeknight, it'd be after two or three o'clock in the morning when she'd leave my bed, and it was never safe for her to walk to her car parked three or four blocks away, especially at that late hour.

I didn't own an auto, didn't have a rented parking place like most of the other store owners who had cars, so Ellen always had to drive around to find a spot. The French Quarter is jammed with cars night and day and, unless you have a place off the street to park, you're usually out of luck.

"Just give me one good reason, please," I'd plead.

"Because I said I can't. That's reason enough, Millie. I said I can't and that's that. Don't ask me again!"

Not speaking, we'd fly through Slidell, cross the lake, wind our way to the Quarter, and say not one more word. Ellen would stop in front of my gallery, her mouth a grim line, and wait for me to gather my junk from the backseat. "I may call you," she'd throw at me, then she'd take off with a roar. So much for most of our Sunday evenings.

Tonight was going to be different. I studied her profile, waiting for the right words.

In for a penny, in for a pound, I decided. So I blurted, "Just give me one good reason why you can't ever spend the night. Surely your mother wouldn't mind once in a while."

Warming to the subject, like the dimwit I am, I rushed on. "Is it because you have to fix her breakfast? You could leave some biscuits or something she could warm in the microwave, couldn't you?" That was unfair and I knew it.

"Millie, stop." She turned to look at me and I saw her anger. I also saw another expression. She was pleading for me to hush; it was there in her eyes plain as day.

I touched her arm. "It's only because I want you with me. I'm more than just fond of you, Ellen, and I know you care for me. So why can't we have a whole night together now and then?"

"I just spent Friday and Saturday night with you. We hardly took our hands off each other. Doesn't that count?"

"Honey, I'd be happy if I just knew why. It's like you're keeping some big, horrible secret from me, like you don't trust me."

"How can you say that after this weekend?" Tears started. I saw them begin to roll down her face.

I yanked a tissue from the box on the dash and gently patted her cheeks, being careful not to blind her. She was driving, after all. I didn't understand what was happening. Usually she just got pissed off when I nagged her about staying over. I could live with that, but tears were beyond me.

"Why are you crying?" I asked.

"I'm with you every free minute I have," she sniffed. "If that's not enough . . ."

"Whoa!" Backpedaling as fast as I could, I said, "Of course it's enough. I didn't mean to upset you, and I'm not prying or anything" — of course I was prying, we both knew it — "but sometimes I just wish you could be with me more than you are, that's all."

"I can stay until about eight tonight. Will that satisfy you?"

Satisfy me? Satisfy my curiosity or my carnality? Which did she mean?

"Yes," I answered. Whichever, I'd have her with me for another few hours. I stroked her thigh. "Yes," I said again, recognizing her slow smile. She had stopped me cold by offering bed instead of answers. I moved my hand farther up her thigh, feeling the faint tingle between my own legs become a flush of heat. Yes, as always, bed would satisfy.

"Get a move on, then, or we'll spend all the time looking for a parking place," I urged.

Extraordinary luck! We found a spot only half a

block down from my gallery. Slamming the outside door shut behind us, we almost ran up my spiral stairway, shedding clothes as we went.

At about a quarter to eight she rolled from my side. It was dark outside, and the corner streetlamp was the only light coming through my skylight roof. She leaned on an elbow, her face over mine. "Did this satisfy?" she asked softly.

"Yes."

"I have to dress now."

"I know."

"I'm going downstairs for a quick shower. Do you want anything?"

My tiny kitchen and shower was directly under my sleeping loft, so I figured she meant did I want something to drink.

"Nope," I answered. "You've taken care of my wants."

She stood looking down. "I'm glad to hear that," she said.

Then, bending to give me a quick kiss, she asked, "Are you happy now?"

"Ummm."

"Can I take that for a yes?"

"Ummm."

I found it hard to sleep that night. Why couldn't she stay overnight with me? "My mother needs care," she'd said. "I have to be at the school by seven, you know, so I need to be home in the morning." Pretty lame, I thought, but I usually didn't try to pin her down, figuring she'd tell me when she was ready. Like with Lou, I didn't ask questions, I just accepted. Until lately, that is.

Another thing that was beginning to nag at me was the pattern of our lovemaking. I tried to remember back to the beginning, but it was sort of hazy. I do recall how fine it was to teach her what to do and how to do it. I didn't mind going over the same lesson time and time again.

Mostly I made love to her, trying whatever I could think of to excite her. Sometimes I had the feeling that sex was all she wanted from me, sex and nothing more. I wanted to call it making love, but it was beginning not to feel like it.

More times than not I would hold her after she came, forgetting my own needs in the pride I felt in arousing her to orgasm. She did make love to me, but her enthusiasm wasn't as great. Was it my task to service her occasionally and then, after successfully completing that, get up and go, my job finished?

Except for this weekend, that is. As I finally drifted into sleep, I thought about the suitcase, the clothes, and the letter. Ellen had been sexually hotter than I'd ever seen her. She had hugged me, kissed me, and nearly sucked me dry. My last conscious thought was of Chicago, where Ellen, on a studio couch, was making passionate love to a faceless woman.

Two calls were on my answering machine phone when I checked Monday morning. One from Lou and one from Miss Leona. I had an agreement with the Gaudet twins, who had the shop two doors from mine. When I was doing pastels from my spot outside the ornate iron railing that enclosed Jackson Square, one of the ladies would sit in my shop and talk with potential customers about my paintings displayed on the gallery walls. Everything was clearly marked, so whichever twin was shop-sitting for me could make the sale, do the paperwork and the packaging, and hold the money for me.

In return, I paid generously and was on call for them whenever they needed a strong back or whatever. They were in their seventies and painted French Quarter scenes on slate for sale to tourists. Their tiny shop was filled with Louisiana knick-knacks, things that sold for a couple of bucks. I don't think they needed money, just that they'd owned the building forever, lived upstairs in a rather large apartment with a balcony, and enjoyed the excitement of being a part of the famous Quarter.

I called Lou first . . . no answer.

Miss Leona answered on the first ring. She'd sold two swamp scenes in oil and one framed pencil sketch of the Saint Louis Cathedral. "I'll stop by on my way to the square this morning," I told her.

It took a few minutes for me to inventory the rolling cart that held my pastels and paper and money box. I sat on a tall, folding deck-type chair when I did portraits, so I loaded that on top of the cart along with my huge umbrella. I filled my thermos with lemon drink, locked my gallery door, and pushed my way down Decatur Street to the iron fence.

Each sidewalk artist, as we're called, has an appointed spot on the fence. My space was on Chartres Street, which was closed to vehicular traffic, and directly across from the Saint Louis Cathedral, the Cabildo, and the Presbytère. On the part of the sidewalk and fence that was mine, I arranged my cart and chair, put out another chair for the person sitting for a portrait, set up my umbrella, and hung my framed samples on the iron posts behind me. I was instantly in business.

That Monday after arranging my work space and touching base with my artist neighbors, I walked back to Dumaine Street to see the twins. There was no need to worry about anything being stolen from my cart because my neighbors, artists like me, would keep a sharp eye on my stuff.

I settled accounts with Miss Leona, sipped a cup of café au lait with the two of them, and used their phone to call Lou again. I got a busy signal. I had forgotten to bring my mobile phone, so I went back to the shop for it.

I had figured out a pretty neat way to run a gallery and do portraits on the square at the same time. When I was on the square, people were welcome to enter my gallery to look at my paintings hanging on the walls and displayed on easels around the room. One of the twins, both knowledgeable in art, would greet them.

If the potential customer felt the need to talk with the artist, Miss Leona or Miss Marie would phone me, and I'd get there in about three minutes.

If I was doing a portrait and couldn't stop, the customer could wait on a comfortable chair in air-conditioned splendor, or make an appointment for later. I hadn't missed more than a couple of sales since I'd been on my own in the Quarter.

I had already done a twelve-by-fourteen portrait of an adorable eight-year-old boy and was stashing my cash box back in the cart when Lou appeared. She looked like hell. It was a look I'd seen before.

I didn't greet her; I just pointed to the low chair, settled myself in my high one, and lifted my eyebrows in an invitation to speak. It took a couple of minutes of staring at the ground before she cleared her throat and looked up at me.

"She's gone."

I didn't need to ask who was gone. "Gee, Lou," I said in sympathy. "I'm sorry to hear that."

"I kept asking her what did she want, but she'd never say."

"Are you sure she's gone? Maybe just pouting is all." Knowing Peaches I could imagine the pouting because I'd seen it many times.

Lou shrugged, twisting her fingers together. "No, not pouting, Millie. Gone. She's gone."

The inevitability of Peaches being gone one day was a fact Ellen and I had discussed. "Poor Lou," Ellen had said. "Poor, sweet Lou. Why do you think this happens to her?"

I had told her a little about Lou's love life after we'd been unwilling listeners to one of her quarrels with Peaches. "What do you suppose is wrong?" Ellen had asked speculatively. "Could sex have anything to do with it?"

"I have no idea. Lou does seem to pick super-feminine women, and maybe they expect too much sex or," I had added lamely, "maybe Lou doesn't want enough or doesn't do it to their satis- faction, or something." I really wasn't comfortable talking about Lou behind her back.

Ellen had ended that conversation by letting me

44

demonstrate that I knew how to do it right. Today, however, Ellen was not around.

I closed my cart and told Lou to come with me; we'd talk over coffee at the Café du Monde. Wending our way around the few tourists who were just beginning to window-shop the area around the square, we found an empty table, ordered coffee, then sat staring at each other.

"Do you want to talk about what happened, Lou?"

She shrugged, brushing powdered sugar off the table with her hand. "Guess so," she said softly. She stared over my shoulder at the street, not meeting my eyes, her mouth a grim line.

"You don't have a clue?" I urged. "Didn't she say?"

Our coffee came. Our table was wiped, and I paid with change from my pocket. Then I watched Lou add four heaping spoons of sugar to her cup.

"Lou," I said, "I don't think you have to give me all the details, just that you might feel better if you talked. Maybe it'd help you figure out what happened." Heaven knows I didn't want details; a simple outline would be sufficient, just enough for Lou to get some of it off her chest.

She stirred her coffee absently, still not meeting my eyes. "Well, I guess I do know why, Millie." Finally coming to a decision, she met my gaze. "Peaches wasn't satisfied with me in bed. She didn't really want a woman, anyway. She wanted a man. At least that's what she said."

I didn't know what to say so I kept quiet, aware of the flush of heat in my face and neck. I watched Lou add another spoon of sugar to her cup.

45

"No matter what I did, she wasn't ever happy." This was said in a very low tone, Lou's gaze centered on her coffee cup.

I waited in the silence that followed Lou's statement, again not knowing what to say. I cleared my throat, stared at the traffic beginning to clog Decatur Street, took a long swallow from my cup, and asked, "Is this a permanent thing or will she be back in time for supper, do you think?"

"No, not back ever unless she decides she didn't take enough with her when she left. She even snatched up the money from the suitcase."

"You mean the thousand dollars we found Saturday?" For some reason this stirred a flash of anger. That money didn't belong to Peaches and she had no right to take it.

"Yeah, I had emptied my pockets on the dresser and it was there in plain sight. She said she'd earned it." Lou stared at her cup. "You see, it's not the money exactly. It's what she said. Like I had to pay . . ."

"Well damn it all," I interrupted, "She didn't have anything to do with that suitcase or the money! That was out-and-out stealing." I was glad the suitcase was safe on my kitchen table. At least, I thought, we still have the letter and the clothes. Why this seemed important to me I'll never know.

"I guess she was stealing, Millie, but I'm so ashamed right now that I don't really care."

"You don't have to be ashamed, Lou. If that's the way it was going, maybe you're better off." Good sense told me not to say too much against Peaches; she might come back when the money was gone.

Lou stared at her cup for a long minute. "Well, I

46

gotta go. Thanks, Millie." She stood, dropped a bill on the table, and walked away.

I crossed Decatur, walked around the square to my spot, set up my easel again, and sat staring across at the Cathedral doors.

Chapter 5

Monday is often kind of slow unless there's a convention. While waiting for my first customer, I did a charcoal of the Cathedral on eight-by-ten and a larger pastel of Pirate's alley showing both the Cabildo and the Cathedral. What I didn't sketch was the drunk, asleep, sprawled on the ground with his back against the Cabildo wall. A urine smell permeated the alley day and night, but I didn't think it should be a part of my drawing, even if I could have included it somehow.

I had started the morning with a glow from the

night before but, as I sat over coffee with Lou, it had begun to fade. Lou is my best friend, and I hated seeing her so down.

Drawing finished, I signed my name and sprayed the paper to fix the colors. Intending to frame it later, I began sliding it into a vertical partition of my cart. I could get more for it in a frame.

"Is that for sale?"

"This drawing?" I asked, holding up the sketch so the morning shadows from the fence didn't compete with the blacks and grays on the paper.

"Yes, we've been watching you draw for a while, and my wife and I like your work. Does it have a price?"

I told him, he looked at his wife, she nodded and handed him a traveler's check, which he signed and handed to me. I kept my smile until they were well past the corner of Saint Peter Street, then I sat back in my chair, check still in hand, and started thinking about Ellen. I wondered why we always had to meet at my place and then only to make love.

The love part was entirely to my liking, but we never went anyplace except to the Gulf Coast on weekends. Weekday mornings her mother needed Ellen to be home to help get the day started. I could understand that. A graduate student from the university stayed over on weekends so Ellen could be with me.

I knew she wouldn't call until Wednesday or Thursday. "I have lesson plans, laundry, and a million other things to do after a weekend with you. You have to give me some time, darling. I have a job, you know, and then there's Mother."

Knowing all that didn't make me any less

lonesome. Sighing, I stuck the check in my cash box. It was going to be a slower Monday than usual from the looks of it.

At noon I closed the cart and walked back to my shop. Miss Leona was sitting primly on the love seat, a decorating-type magazine open on her lap. She looked up. "Nothing much today, Millie. Even the mailman passed without stopping."

"Well, can't win them all. Want me to get you a sandwich from the grocery?"

"No, thank you. Sister is bringing something very soon. You run along, dear."

First I headed for the toilet, passing my tiny kitchen table on the way. The suitcase was where Ellen and I had dumped it as we had rushed up to the bed last night. I paused. Turning on my faux Tiffany overhead lamp, I sat at the table and opened the straps that held the lid closed. Again, when I lifted the lid, a faint sweet odor reached my nose. Testing, I leaned over and drew in another breath, but the faint scent had disappeared.

We had repacked the few items taken from the case yesterday, so I began searching the entire contents to see if I could find anything to identify the owner, something we'd missed. Lunch could wait a few minutes.

I examined each garment carefully, shaking it out before refolding, but I could find no identifying marks. I read the letter again, looked at the picture, then scrutinized the train ticket for a name or address that we might have missed. Nothing. It wasn't until I repacked a dainty handkerchief that I saw initials delicately hand stitched on one lacy edge. A small *M* in the center, then a small *T*.

MTL. Did the *M* stand for Mary? Mazie? Margaret? The *T* was the initial of her middle name, probably, and could also be any name at all. The large *L*, I supposed, was her last name and could be Leger, Landrieu, Louis or whatever. But at least, I thought, the initials were an identity we could fit to a proper name if we ever found one. Unaccountably, I felt sad.

At that moment I realized I wanted very much to find out what had happened . . . why the ticket to Chicago was never used . . . why the money was never taken out and spent . . . why the clothes were still neatly folded in what looked to be an expensive suitcase . . . and why it was hidden in a rumrunner's hideaway on the Mississippi coast for sixty years.

I closed the case with a sigh. Whispering, I said, "Whoever you were, I have a feeling what happened to you wasn't what you planned."

"Millie, are you calling?"

"No, I'm just talking to myself." I lifted the suitcase, placed it on the floor, and shoved it under the table next to the wall so that it wouldn't show unless someone stooped to look for it. There wasn't any reason for doing this except that I felt like it.

After calling the grocery to order my muffuletta, I took my time walking around the corner to Decatur. Even though it was a clear, sunny day, the usual horde of tourists weren't crawling like ants on sugar so I strolled, looking into shop windows as if I hadn't seen them before.

The sidewalks around the square are made of

thick slate rectangles. They're gray, large, hand cut, and have been there for a very long time. I don't know how long, but at least since the equestrian statue of General Jackson was put into place before the Civil War. I enjoyed imagining grand ladies with their sweeping gowns and gentlemen in top hats taking their Sunday promenade on these same slate slabs. The Pontalba apartments front the square on two sides, Saint Peter and Saint Ann streets, and those elegant people could have simply walked out of their doors onto the very slabs I walked on now.

That picture was so intriguing to me that I had sketched it many times, including the Pontalba buildings and General Jackson on his rearing horse, and I sold it each time. Out to see and be seen, the ladies were demure and the gentlemen would bow slightly as they tipped their hats.

My muffuletta was ready, wrapped in butcher paper. I also paid for two small cartons of milk. On the way to the grocery I had an idea, something we could do toward identifying the owner of the suitcase. Both Ellen and I had decided she was probably from New Orleans, so there was a good place to start looking and I knew how to go about it.

I walked through the iron gates into the square and picked a bench by the sidewalk, one that wasn't already occupied by a sleeping person. There may have been room, but I didn't fancy trying to eat with somebody's feet in my lap. Anyway, I expected company.

Micah wasn't long in coming. I had taken two huge bites, was still chewing the second one, when Micah sat on the bench next to me. He waited for me to swallow then said, "Not too busy today, is it?"

I took a gulp of milk. "Well, you know how it is some Mondays."

Micah looked at the sandwich half that I had rewrapped and the carton of milk on the seat next to it. "It's yours, Micah," I said. "You know I can never finish a whole one. The milk is for you, too."

"Thanks, Millie." He opened the milk, took several huge swallows, then bit into the sandwich. We'd found that both of us liked olives and provolone, so when the grocery made my muffuletta they crowded it with olive salad and cheese, among other things. "Man, this is good," Micah said appreciatively.

We sat in companionable silence, each concentrating on the food, not talking, finishing at the same time. We put our trash in the bag from the grocery and sat, not looking at anything in particular. Finally I said, "Want to earn a few bucks?"

"You know I do." Micah nodded, his blue eyes wide and his mouth — what I could see of it under the beard — stretched in a grin that showed even, white teeth.

"Okay, then. I'd like for you to go to the library for me. I want to know if there was a young woman reported missing sometime in nineteen thirty-three. I don't know her name, but her initials are *MTL*."

"Do you have a closer date than just the year?"

"Nope, I may not even have the year right. Matter of fact, she may not be mentioned in the paper at all." Micah looked puzzled. "It's a kind of mystery and I don't have time to spend looking in old records and stuff. You're the first person I've asked. I figured microfilm at the library would be a good place to start."

Micah smiled ruefully. "I'd like to do it for you,

53

but I'm not exactly dressed to go to a library. The only one that would have anything on microfilm is the main one downtown, and I look like a tramp, Millie." He shook his head. "These are the only clothes I own."

To me, it wasn't strange that he'd think of his appearance. Micah was as ragged as the other homeless-type people. From his bearing and speech I suspected that he probably had a Ph.D. in rocket science or some such. Why he was wandering around the Quarter was anybody's guess.

I remembered two months back when we'd shared a bench. As I had been about to trash what was left of my sandwich Micah had asked for it. Silently, I had handed it to him before I got up and left. Next day, when I went into the square to eat, I looked for him. That time I had half a muffuletta, which he took with a shy "Thank you, ma'am."

It was many days before we started talking but than we became as comfortable with each other as longtime friends.

I looked at him and frowned. "You do look kind of dull, Micah. If I could fit you out in something better, would you go?"

"Sure." He didn't look as if going to the main library and using their files would faze him in the least.

"Well, let's go to the Goodwill place on Toulouse. You won't look like a banker, but you'll be neat."

I wasn't trying to shame him, but we both knew that his appearance identified him as one of the city's homeless. Very visible, they wander the Quarter and the city's business section. Panhandling and sleeping in doorways make them generally undesirable.

I called Miss Leona to tell her where I'd be and closed my cart. We walked to Toulouse Street and the used-clothing store. Micah found a pair of faded jeans that fit, a newly pressed white dress shirt, a belt, and a pair of running shoes, almost new. We even picked a pair of black socks.

Altogether, I spent eight dollars. To my way of thinking it was worth every penny.

As we left the store with Micah's bundle of clothes he turned to me. "Millie, I haven't had a bath in a while." He shrugged. "There aren't any public bathhouses around here."

I thought for a moment. "Guess you'll have to shower at my place."

I introduced Micah to Miss Leona, who was as gracious as if I'd introduced Prince Charles. He took her hand saying, "I'm honored to meet you, Miss Leona." His little half bow pleased her tremendously.

After explaining that Micah was going to use the shower, I headed back to my spot on the fence. I was doing a pastel of a mother and her two children when it occurred to me that I was trusting someone who could steal me blind and I didn't even know his full name or anything about him. At least, I figured, I could sketch his likeness for the police.

"So, you're from Minnesota. I've never been there." This was a continuation of the conversation I'd started when the woman decided she'd like a souvenir portrait to show the folks back home. Getting people to talk took some of the stiffness away when they posed. I didn't want them sitting like marble statues. It wasn't all that easy for me to talk to strangers, but it kept them relaxed.

The woman described her home, her neighbors,

her husband, the birth of her two children, and the plans to head to Florida when they were finished in New Orleans. My mind sketched Ellen in vivid colors as she offered herself to me this weekend. I could feel her, wet and slippery, hips thrusting, her thigh grinding between my legs as she moved in quick, short jerks.

Ellen had climaxed, I had climaxed, and remembering caused me to press the paper so hard my pastel broke, half falling to the ground and the other half grinding into the paper. The woman hadn't noticed a thing. She kept talking, and I kept working but breathing like a race horse on the final stretch.

Micah's hair was wet, but he looked quite presentable. "Think they'll throw me out?" he asked.

"Naw, you look like you belong in a library. All you need is a notebook, a pen, and plenty of patience."

"Where exactly do you want me to start, Millie? Shall I do the obituaries first? The police reports? What?" Obviously, he knew something about research.

"All I know is that a woman, probably very early twenties, had a ticket to go to Chicago in July of nineteen thirty-three. We found her suitcase, still packed, and her train ticket unused. What I want is for you to see if something showed up in the paper around that time."

Micah looked shamefaced for a second or two, his right hand digging into his pocket. "Millie, I don't have bus fare," he said.

"Heck, I forgot." I handed him a five. "This'll get

you there and back. I'll be in my shop. Come there when you finish."

Watching him walk away down Decatur, I wondered why he was living hand-to-mouth. It seemed to me that he was an educated person. I didn't understand Micah and I didn't understand Ellen.

I toyed with the idea of calling Ellen this evening to tell her about Micah, but she'd made me promise not to call her at home. "I'll call you, darling, when I'm free." I figured it was because of her mother. Ah, well, if that's the way it had to be, I'd live with it.

By the end of the day my sales had picked up. Feeling good, I wheeled the cart back to my shop and settled with Miss Leona, who had volunteered to wash Micah's soiled clothes.

"I'll have them here in the morning, dear. I like that young man," she said.

Chapter 6

It was late when I heard someone tapping on my door. Because a lot of tourists wander the Quarter at night, I always left the front gallery room lighted. They might see an interesting painting and come back the next day. If I wanted privacy, I would close the blinds over the door and the plate glass display window; otherwise I left it open. It was through the glass that I saw Micah, hands stuffed in his pockets, shoulders hunched, grin spread from ear to ear.

Not waiting for the door to open fully, I asked, "Got something, did you?"

He nodded. "Yep."

I moved him to the love seat, sat in the nearest chair, and leaned forward. "Well, what?"

"You want it in bits and pieces or shall I start at the beginning?"

I was about to pop but I said, "I want it all!"

"Okay." He cleared his throat. "At first I thought I'd start with the *Times Picayune* in January of thirty-three, but that didn't get me anyplace. Prohibition ended that year, in November, so I started looking backward from then. Don't ask me why."

"Ha, that was a pretty good guess, Micah. I hadn't told you we found her suitcase in an underground room dug into the Mississippi coast . . . a room packed with crates and crates of liquor. It had occurred to me that prohibition had something to do with it and, since we found the booze and the suitcase together, why not?"

Micah nodded. "I'm a fast reader, so I went through the paper pretty quickly. It was in early September that the unidentified body of a young woman was found near the Pontchartrain spillway. Some crabbers caught her with their hook. She was tied hand and foot and weighted with a hunk of concrete from the seawall."

"Ah, no," I said sadly, hoping the woman wasn't our *MTL*.

"She was badly decomposed, but she had dark hair and was rather small, probably around twenty years old. Hers wasn't the only body washed ashore those days, but it was the only young female." He paused, shaking his head.

"Micah, I'll never eat another crab, so help me."

People baited crab nets with any fleshy edible available, and crabs swarmed over whatever they could eat, picking and tearing.

"Of course you will," Micah said. "Do you have any idea what your lady looked like?"

I answered softly, "Small, dark hair, around twenty years old."

"I guess there are plenty who'd answer to that description, so hang in, Millie, there's more."

"All bad, I guess."

"Depends on how you look at it. You just wanted an identity, didn't you? I think I have one for you."

He took a piece of paper from his pocket. Turning so that the light shone full on his hands he began, "On July twenty-fifth a young woman identified as Marléne T. Livaudias was pictured on the front page. The headline said, 'Heiress Missing.' Apparently she had dropped from sight several days before. A few articles of clothing were also missing. There had been no ransom note or phone calls. I followed up on it because her initials matched the ones you gave me."

Micah looked up, took a deep breath, and continued. "According to the *Picayune*, Marléne was the niece of Michael Livaudias who ran the rackets in New Orleans. He was into prostitution, numbers, even drugs. He was a rich kid gone wrong according to an editorial. The rest of the family was wealthy New Orleans society. The paper probably played it up because of the uncle's connection to racketeering."

"Do you think the uncle had something to do with her disappearance?"

"I don't know what to think, Millie. It seems kind of far-fetched." He thought for a minute, his gaze fixed on my oil painting of a heron rookery in the

Manchac swamp. Finally, leaning forward on the love seat, he asked, "You found a suitcase in a rum-runner's hideaway? Her uncle ran booze, and there were reported to be dozens of manmade hiding places along the Gulf Coast and the Mississippi River. Maybe there is a connection."

"Those weren't the dark ages back then. People didn't have computers or mobile phones, but they could identify bodies from dental records, couldn't they?"

Micah nodded. "I'm sure they could."

"Well, didn't the coroner check dental records to see if the body they found was Marléne Livaudias?"

"I'll have to go back tomorrow, Millie. Now that I know a little more about your mystery lady, I'll see what I can learn from the coroner's records. There was a ten-thousand-dollar reward for any information, and that was a lot of money in those days."

"It was never claimed?"

"Not that I found."

"She was missing at the end of July, and a body was found in September, right?" At Micah's nod I added, "Didn't anybody connect the two?"

"Don't know. Have to do some more digging."

I sighed, more than a little irritated. Here was a woman missing from New Orleans, the person I assumed was her lover waiting for her in Chicago, and her suitcase stored underground in Mississippi with a million gallons of booze. Did her uncle kill her? That was possible, if I recalled what I'd read about gangsters during prohibition. But why her?

"You'll try again tomorrow?" I asked, hoping he'd agree.

"Sure I will, Millie. I'm curious too."

I handed him ten dollars. "Here's bus fare and lunch money. Think you need more?"

"No. But is it okay if I collect my clothes from Miss Leona tomorrow morning? And may I shower again?"

That sounded reasonable to me. I knew the broken-down shelter over on Saint Louis street had facilities for the homeless, but it didn't have a very good reputation. I could understand why Micah wouldn't want to use their showers.

"I'm on the square around eight-thirty, and Miss Leona opens this place around nine. She'll let you in."

Micah nodded and pocketed the money. I let him out after thanking him and meaning every word.

After crawling into bed, I began to think about Micah. I had bought clothes and let him use my shower and toilet, but there was nothing personal in it. It was just expedient. Micah wouldn't misunderstand.

There was some kind of affair taking place on the river, and spotlights were crisscrossing the black night. Shadows flickered into brightness as the lights crossed my skylight, reminding me of Ellen and a similar evening some time ago.

As I had made love to her, I'd timed my fingers to slide inside as the overhead brightened. Then, as the light faded I withdrew, poised to thrust again when her face was revealed to me.

After a minute or so she caught the rhythm and

slowed the movement of her hips to match the flashes of light. Like slow dancing, we moved together until her breathing began to escalate and I felt the cadence change. She caught my wrist and guided my hand into frenzied movement. Breathing hard, I pushed faster, feeling her legs widen and her moisture gushing as she climaxed.

At that same moment the glass had brightened and her eyes had opened. We stayed like that, face-to-face, neither speaking. When the brightness faded she held my hand between her legs, and my fingers, moving in her velvety warmth, began the dance again.

Sleep did not come easily after reliving sex with Ellen. I wanted her in bed with me doing the wild things she had done this past weekend. There was an ache between my legs and I was wet.

I had choices. I could lie awake thinking about Ellen and save my sexual energy until she called. Or I could direct my thoughts to *MTL*, try to make the mystery less mysterious. I thought about my options and made a decision. Raising my knees, I moved my hands under the sheet and felt the first tingle as my fingers touched moist flesh.

Morning came too soon. I showered, dressed, checked my cart, counted my money, and made a bank deposit. I walked out to Decatur, crossed, and took a seat at the Morning Call.

"The usual," I said to Frank as he leaned to wipe my table.

"How're things, Millie?" he asked cheerfully.

" 'Bout the same, I think, except for the light show last night. What was it?"

"Some new thing at the Mint . . . they've opened part of the basement, I think, as a cabaret and dance floor."

"We'll go dancing there some night. Just you and me," I said.

Frank snorted, a kind of horsey neigh except more high-pitched. He was young and gay with a stable of lovers. I'd never seen him with the same stud twice.

He leaned, still circling the tabletop with a damp cloth, and whispered, "Last night I met the most gorgeous man. We fell in love the minute our eyes met."

I honestly didn't want to hear about eyes making contact across a crowded room, or any other kind of room, so I stopped the circling motion of his hand. "Frank, I'm in a hurry this morning. Will you tell me later?" I knew he would. I had become his confidant since he'd started work in the coffee house.

The first time he had waited on me, our eyes did meet across the round marble table, and we each knew the other at once. As I gnawed my beignets, scattering powdered sugar, he had wiped the table twice.

"My name is Frank," he'd whispered as I drained my cup, "and my new lover is sitting next to the post." He had gazed fondly at a young man drinking café au lait, elbows propped on the table. How many times since had he pointed out "new lovers" to me?

"Very nice," I'd said, not at all comfortable with such instant intimacy. I didn't give a damn about his lovers, new or old. As time passed things had changed. Now, if I didn't listen avidly, at least I listened. Frank was very young and very lonesome, and I had become his friend.

I studied the sleepy-eyed young man sipping coffee and wolfing down a beignet. I noticed his hand-me-down clothes, scuffed shoes, and hair long overdue for a wash.

"Send him over and I'll do his portrait for you," I said. This wasn't as generous as it sounded. When drawing from life, I'd always collect a crowd of curious tourists. Chances were that one of them would decide to get a portrait done. Having Frank's new lover sit for me would generate business. Frank must have had a gallery of unframed portraits.

I asked Frank to tell his new lover not to hang around if I already had a customer. I paid my bill, collected my cart, and wheeled it around to Chartres Street and my space across from the Cathedral.

They say it takes one to know one, so I was sure the two women coming out of the Cathedral were lesbians. There was just something in the way they walked or dressed or combed their hair or whatever that was as clear to me as if they had been branded with an *L* on their foreheads. Especially in the summer, the Quarter was host to many, many women who strolled the streets two-by-two on their sensible, flat shoes, camera dangling, no purse in sight.

It was obvious to me that these two were "together," and I watched them with a certain sadness. In addition to a couple of popular male stars, I had pastels of Garbo, Anne Murray, and k. d. lang displayed on the fence behind me. It caught their attention. They walked over to my space, stood not too close, and examined each portrait carefully. They also examined me. I passed inspection because the shorter of the two moved closer. "How long does it take?" she asked.

I told her, explaining the small discount if I did both. She stepped back and began a discussion with the tall one, head tilted, hands in motion. When the tall one nodded, she stepped back to me. "Will you do my friend first?"

"I can do both of you in one portrait if you'd like." This was a standard offer, but they stared back at me as if I'd asked them to pose nude. "Lots of people do it that way," I explained lamely. What I should have said was, "Look, I'm a sister and I know how it is, so if you'd like something of the two of you together to hang over your bed, I'm your person."

The short one, eyebrows raised, looked at the tall one. They both turned to me again. The tall one smiled and nodded, the short one beamed, and they stepped into the shade of my umbrella.

Chapter 7

Tuesday had been a good day. Before noon, Miss Leona sold three swamp scenes in oil and one large clown portrait. I didn't have anything in reserve because I'd spent weekends doing carpentry work at the camp instead of painting backup oils for the gallery walls. I would have to paint that weekend. When Ellen called me on the mobile phone in the afternoon, I told her I could knock out half a dozen swamps (my basic design) in two days but not if I went to the coast. "Can't you take your stuff and do it there?" she asked. "I thought we'd plan something special, like last weekend. Wouldn't you like that?"

"Yes, I'd like that," I answered. "You know I would. But, honey, I also have to eat, and I don't make any money when there's nothing in my shop to sell."

"I see," she said. "Well, if you'd rather have paint than have me, we can just forget the coast."

"Wait, please understand. I don't have a steady income like you. I have to paint things in order to sell things. It'll just be this one weekend, I promise." I heard the whine in my voice and hated myself for it.

"We'll call it off, if that's what you want."

"My god, Ellen. Call what off?"

"The weekend," she said. "Us," she said.

"Are you kidding? Please tell me you're kidding." My voice had risen a couple of octaves. People passing could hear every word. Each time she threatened to break off with me, I'd fall to my knees, begging. I fell now.

Calming my voice and speaking into her silence, I said, "Ellen, I know you can't mean that. Please, honey, I don't want to quarrel with you. Come over tonight and we'll talk."

"No," she said, "I'll come tomorrow." Then she hung up.

I gnawed my thumbnail, thinking. If I closed my cart and spent the rest of the afternoon painting in the shop, I could get a good start on filling the gallery walls. I probably wouldn't earn more than forty dollars or so the rest of the day on the square, but I could get ahead on several hundred dollars' worth of oils. I closed my cart, nodded to my neighbors, and rolled my belongings back to Dumaine Street.

Miss Leona had planned to stay until closing, whether I was in the shop or not, so I set up in the little painting room next to the gallery, turned on all the lights, and started blocking in canvas. While I sketched charcoal outlines I tried to make sense of my conversation with Ellen.

I felt that I had been the one to pursue Ellen, but had it actually been that way? No, several times she had showed up at the fence just as I was about to close. She would smile and we'd talk. I thought she was straight. I thought she was just passing by. When I finally gathered enough courage to ask her to go out to dinner with me, she had accepted instantly. On the second date she had been the one to offer sex — before I had even gathered enough nerve to brush hands, although I was almost desperate to touch her.

"Good night, dear," Miss Leona called. "I'll see you tomorrow."

" 'Night," I said as Miss Leona hung the Closed sign and quietly shut the door behind her.

"Coming," I called a moment later.

"I think I have it," Micah said as we sat.

"Wait, let me close the blinds." I was eager to learn what he'd discovered but sometimes, in spite of the sign, tourists would knock to come in if they saw people inside.

"Now, tell me," I urged, pulling my chair so that it faced the love seat.

"I'm going to tell you a story, what I think

happened. Of course this is speculation on my part, but" — Micah spread his hands, palms up— "I'm probably more right than wrong."

"Okay," I agreed. "What do you think happened?"

"It was murder, no doubt about that. The woman drowned. She was bound hand and foot, weighted, and tossed into the lake. There may have been other injuries — the coroner couldn't say because of the crabs — but she was alive when she went into the water."

"Dear God," I said. "What a way to die."

"She's your *MTL*. Dental records were checked, and the identification was positive."

"Why did that happen to her, Micah?" I squeezed my hands together, feeling a heavy sadness that almost brought tears. I had seen her neatly folded clothes, whiffed the sweet scent of her perfume, known why she was headed to Chicago. I thought of Helen waiting for the lover who never came.

"Marléne was an honest-to-goodness heiress," Micah said. "She was in her senior year at Newcomb College when her name was on a published list of women arrested for dancing in a lesbian bar in the Gentilly section of town. The names and addresses were printed in the morning paper, but her name was omitted from the evening edition."

"Money talks, huh?"

"It did that time. Anyway, her name wasn't on the list of Newcomb graduates that year, so she must have dropped out of school. It was around then that bodies began floating to the top, and I do mean floating. There was a gang war, each side shooting at the other, and mass extinction took place. I think, from the looks of it, that Marléne got caught in the middle."

"How could she? She wasn't a gangster."

"No, but her uncle was. The way she dropped from sight makes me think she was snatched and killed as a lesson or a warning to her uncle."

"Oh, no, Micah! They wouldn't do that!"

"From what I've read, there are more people wearing cement shoes in the river and in the lake than there are walking around town."

"But she was so young."

"All the better from their point of view I guess. She's in Metairie Cemetery, in one of those aboveground vaults. I saw fresh flowers, so somebody still cares."

"Who, I wonder? She's been dead sixty years."

"I asked the attendant about that. He doesn't know except that a florist puts out flowers every month, and a woman shows up with fresh red roses every once in a while. Marléne's parents are in there with her, so maybe it's some relative doing it. The florist couldn't tell me anything."

"Did she have brothers or sisters?"

"No, the entire estate went to Newcomb College."

"Micah, I have to think about this." My head was so full of ugly pictures that I hated to close my eyes. "Will you come to the square at noon?" I asked. "I'll settle up with you then, okay? Unless you need money now?"

Micah shook his head. "No, I'm fine, Millie. Actually, I've enjoyed doing research for you. It was nice to use skills I haven't touched for a long time."

Whatever that meant, I was glad when the door

closed behind him. I left the blinds down, turned out the gallery lights, and went back to my sketching. If I wanted the weekend with Ellen, I'd best get my painting done before Saturday. It was Tuesday, and Ellen would come the next night, so I wouldn't be doing any work then. That left Thursday and Friday. I fixed a glass of lemonade and took up my charcoal again.

Wednesday, after I'd put away my cart, I changed the bedsheets, took a shower, and sat in the gallery reading Miss Leona's magazine. I also had put away the signs of my working on canvas. If my working had been what riled Ellen, then I wanted no signs of it where she could see. I'm not only shy, I'm a coward.

Ellen's expression was neutral when she greeted me. I lowered the blinds and held out my arms. Slowly, somewhat reluctantly, she walked to me. I didn't kiss her, I just held my arms around her, my body pressing.

"I'm so glad you're here," I said, nuzzling her neck.

"I'm glad you're glad, but I almost didn't come."

"Look," I said, "about this weekend . . ."

"No, don't say anything. If you can't go, then you can't go. I'll just have to live with it." I felt her shrug.

"But we can go. We'll paint, tape Sheetrock, swim, eat, and we'll make love for hours. How's that sound?"

She shrugged again. "All of the above are okay with me."

My arms were still around her and she hadn't made any move to pull away, so I tightened my hold saying, "Would you like to grab a sandwich or shall we go upstairs?" Her answer was to pull away slightly. She leaned so that we could kiss. As usual, the tingle started when her tongue touched mine.

I turned out the lights and was unbuttoned before we reached the loft floor. She was wearing a dress that I pulled over her head, a bra that I unclasped and dropped to the floor, briefs that she stepped out of with my help, and shoes that she kicked into the corner with a flick of her foot.

Feeling her heat as I ran my hands over her body caused my breathing to quicken. I knelt, took her breasts in my hands and, with my tongue, wrote her name in wet letters on the smooth flesh of her stomach.

After a moment, I forgot how to spell *Ellen* so I licked what I could, finally sinking to my heels so that her pubic hair was within reach. I wrapped my arms low around her hips and made a trail down as far as my tongue could reach.

I was digging my way through her silky brush when I became conscious of her movement away from me. "What? What's the matter?" I choked.

"You're still dressed."

"Only for a minute," I breathed, shedding as fast as I could. I intended to return to my previous activity, but Ellen had other plans.

"I want to fuck you," she said. The glint in her eyes was positively wicked. With her urging, I lay on

73

the mattress, legs spread, waiting. "First," she said, "I want you to feel me. Feel what happens when you touch me like that." She was kneeling at my side, taking quick little breaths.

I slid my hand between her legs, heard her gasp as my fingers began searching through moisture. "Oh, Millie!" she breathed as my fingers moved. "Please." Did that mean stop or continue? When I felt her knees move apart, giving me room enough to slide inside her, I knew the answer. She was very wet, wet and slippery and ready.

I sat up, my finger still in place, and I said, "No, I'm going to fuck you, my dear." I pushed her, unresisting, to her back, pulled out the one finger, and inserted more. She shifted, as if I had touched some painful spot, but she didn't pull away.

We rolled together. She was wild, urging more, crying for me to sink into her faster, faster. With my thumb I stroked her clitoris, with my mouth I sucked her breasts, and with my fingers I fucked her. She came suddenly, her body arching, thighs rigid, and my hand was caught inside, held there by the grip of her legs.

We lay together, my arm under her head, and we silently contemplated the skylight. Finally, she lifted on an elbow and peered at my face. "I can't believe I thought of leaving you. I could stop breathing more easily than I could do without you." Her voice was a whisper, almost as if she were talking to herself.

If I hadn't been speechless with desire, I would have questioned this. When she put her head on my breast, slid her hand down my body, and began playing in the moisture that still issued from me, I managed to choke, "Ellen, fuck me now or I'll die."

My intention was to lie quietly, let her have her way. I'd see how inventive she was after last weekend. It would be research, I told myself.

Ellen had learned a lot since we had become lovers, and she had some ideas of her own. With single-minded directness she concentrated on my clitoris, her tongue warm and slippery. I was as still as I could be, my knees stretched wide, hands clenched, mouth open wide to draw in the volume of air I needed. When I began moving, as I had to when I felt the pleasure and the ache beginning to spread in waves throughout my body, Ellen simply quit. She raised her head to look at me. I stared at her over the expanse of my body, and I said those old, familiar words, "Please don't stop!"

I could see her smile. After a moment she touched my clitoris tentatively, touched it with a tiny flick of her tongue, then looked up at me again. I was swollen, my body poised to burst. Her touch was soft, soft yet hard, and her warm mouth was hungry when she again sucked and sucked.

Afterward, we lay in each other's arms, her thigh between my legs, and we watched the skylight glow. "I have something to tell you," I whispered. "Something about our mystery woman."

She almost raised her head, almost but not quite. "What?" she asked.

"I know who she is." I corrected myself. "Was. I know who she was."

"Tell me," she said sleepily.

Chapter 8

Micah didn't wait until noon. I had just finished setting up my cart when he appeared. He walked with me to the coffee stand, held my chair, and did the ordering. A tall, blond waiter served us. Frank wasn't there; didn't even call in, we were told. I wondered about Frank momentarily, then began listening to Micah.

"There wasn't anything in the suitcase that would give you a clue why she was leaving town?" he asked.

I thought for a moment, wondering what I should tell him. Figuring he already knew more than I did, I said, "She was going to Chicago to be with a woman named Helen. That's the only name we have. We think they were lovers." I watched Micah's face, but his expression didn't change. I did notice that his beard had been trimmed, however.

Micah studied his coffee, running his thumb over the cup handle. Finally he said, "I figured something like that."

I carefully licked powdered sugar from my fingers. "Why?"

"Well, the lesbian bar article gave me a clue. The paper said that most of the women picked up that particular night had been arrested there before."

I ground my teeth over that. How unfair! I changed the subject. "Do you think we could try to locate Helen, or her relatives?"

"Millie, sixty years is a long time. If you knew Helen's address, or even her last name, you could try, but there were probably hundreds of women named Helen in Chicago."

I sighed. We had come so far just to be stopped by a blank wall. I smiled at Micah and said, "I really appreciate what you've done. There's no way I could have spared the time even if I had known where to look." I pushed back my chair. "Come on back to the fence with me and we'll settle accounts."

"I'll walk you back, Millie, but there isn't any account to settle. You've been my friend; you haven't tried to pry into my life; you've trusted me; and you'll never know how much that's meant. I think everything's square between us, and it's time for me to hit the road."

"What's that mean?" I asked, handing a couple of bills to the waiter.

"I've been a bum long enough," Micah said. "Doing this for you has made me realize that I'm not cut out to be a transient. I'm going home."

"Home?" I asked.

"Yes, I spent years without a break, in school and then working. I thought I owed myself a long vacation doing nothing, being nobody, and I ended up here. But I haven't been comfortable here, either."

"You're some kind of teacher, aren't you?" I asked.

He laughed, turning to look at me, his blue eyes clear. "Yes," he said, nodding. "A teacher. But, how did you know?

"It was just a wild guess."

"I plan to leave this afternoon. I have enough stashed away to go by bus; as they say, that's the way to see the country." He paused. "I'd like to keep in touch, if that's okay with you."

"Sure." I was as curious as a cat, but if he wanted me to know any more about him he would tell me. He didn't say more and I didn't ask. He did accept thirty dollars. "For food on the way," I explained. We shook hands solemnly, and he walked away, not looking back.

"You going to the camp this weekend?" It was Lou. She sounded like she always did, so I asked if she wanted to eat supper with me.

"I have to work on some oils tonight," I said. "I

also have to eat, so why don't you come around six-thirty? We'll walk to that spaghetti place on Bourbon Street."

"Sounds good to me. I'll be there."

We picked a table close to the wall. I had to brush bread crumbs off my chair, and Lou wiped at the red smears on her side of the tablecloth. "Why the hell don't they use plastic?" she grumbled, easing her weight on the spindly chair.

"This is the only cheap joint in town that doesn't use plastic. They think real cloth gives them class." I smiled at our waiter, who smiled back showing huge, horse teeth in his tiny pink mouth.

He stood waiting, pencil poised. We stared at him. He stared at us. Finally Lou asked, "Do you have menus?"

"I'm sorry," he murmured, clearly not sorry at all. Reaching for the menus on the table behind us, he presented them as if we had committed some ugly breach of etiquette.

Our meal, when it finally came, was delicious spaghetti and daube, served fire hot and with crusty French bread, oven-heated and lathered with butter. "Cholesterol city," Lou grumbled happily, swiping her bread through the gravy. We had pecan pie for dessert and coffee.

Over our second cup of coffee, grudgingly served by our waiter, I told Lou what I knew about Marléne. "We're at an end now, I think, because she and Helen are both dead after all this time. We don't have Helen's last name, so we can't try to trace her. If only Marléne had saved Helen's envelope."

"She's buried in Metairie Cemetery, you say?"

"Uh-huh, with her parents. Micah said a florist leaves fresh flowers on the grave and that sometimes a woman visits and brings flowers."

"You could try to find out who's leaving flowers. Maybe the florist knows something." Lou pushed her empty cup to the center of the table. "The custodian out there may be able to help."

"Don't know, Lou. Micah has already talked with a clerk at the flower shop who could only tell him that the monthly order for fresh flowers had been around forever, but he didn't know whose order it was. Micah said a woman leaves fresh red roses on the grave and has been doing this for a long time, though not at any particular time during the year."

"Doesn't that kind of tell you something?" Lou tapped the table thoughtfully. "Most people buy plastic flowers these days because fresh ones are expensive and they don't last. The woman may be wealthy, you know. Wasn't Marléne supposed to be an heiress?"

"Yes, she actually was. Do you suppose we could go to the cemetery, give the custodian a few bucks, and ask him to call us when the woman shows up? Maybe he could get her number."

"It's worth a try."

We paid our bill, left a generous tip for lousy service, and walked to my shop. During my four years as a street artist, I've gotten to know just about every regular in the Quarter. It isn't in my nature to initiate contact, but I had a smile or a greeting for everyone who spoke to me first.

"Want another cup?" Lou asked when we rounded

Decatur Street. At my nod we crossed and took a table in the back, next to the alley. There were quite a few tourists not paying one bit of attention to us.

Somewhere near, a live band was playing something I'd never heard before and didn't want to hear again. Lou and I hunched over our cups, straining to hear over the noise. I figured we were here for a purpose, and I was right.

"She called," Lou said.

I didn't have to ask who had called. "What did she want?"

"She says she made a mistake." Lou's glance roamed the other tables, finally came to a stop on her cup.

"What do you think, Lou?" I didn't know what Lou thought, but I thought I knew what she wanted.

"When she left, I thought it was a mistake, too. Now I don't know. We hadn't been happy for a long time. Maybe it was the right thing to do . . . leaving me, I mean. Maybe it wasn't a mistake."

I took a quick sip of coffee and touched her wrist with a finger. "Maybe you ought to cool it for a while, see if leaving really was the right thing, and let her know how you feel. Y'all should talk about things and settle the problems before you jump into bed again." Then I remembered that Peaches didn't want a woman, according to Lou. My thinking was that Peaches' money was gone and that Lou was always an easy touch. Peaches probably wanted to restock her purse, then she'd be off again.

It was a full two minutes before Lou spoke. "She called from Hattiesburg. She expects me to pick her

81

up this evening around ten. What should I do, Millie?"

"If you were going to do that, you should have left an hour ago. Honest, Lou, she pulls you around every which way. Don't you think it's time you spent some energy on yourself?"

Somewhere along the line I had stopped being careful what I said about Peaches.

"That's why I haven't left." Her face was grim, lips stretched in a tight line. "And that's why I'm not going to leave. She can wait there forever, as far as I'm concerned!"

"Is there anything I can do?"

"Naw. I'm going home and take the phone off the hook." She stood, her resolve showing in the set of her shoulders. " 'Night, Millie."

I closed the blinds, turned on soft music, and started mixing paint. The phone rang. I had no idea who'd call me that late. "Hello," I said, not taking my eyes off the soft, sunset colors I had put together.

"I'm thinking about you and about last night."

My mouth went dry. What I had wanted a few seconds ago was to get some background paint on canvas. How quickly my needs had changed! Just the sound of her voice made me so horny that sitting was almost painful.

"Where are you?" I asked.

"Home, but I'd like to be with you, in bed." She was whispering, almost as if her hand were covering the mouthpiece.

"Then come over," I urged. I could always paint later.

"No, you know I can't. I just wanted to thank you for last night. It was a wonderful evening."

"If you can't come here, I'll come there! I can get a cab, you know." Failing that, I would run.

"Mother's awake. I have to go now." The line went dead.

"Wait!" I hollered. "Wait!" For a minute I held the phone to my ear, unbelieving. In a spurt of anger I slammed it back on the table.

It occurred to me that Lou wasn't the only one being led around. I remembered that Ellen had made the first move, although I might have if given enough time. She had been so eager, so responsive, so willing to learn how lesbians made love. But I also recalled that our togetherness had been slowly going downhill until last weekend and the suitcase.

When it came right down to it, I would know Ellen in the dark. I knew the feel of her and the smell of her and the taste of her, but I didn't really know her! She seemed to blow hot and cold at the same time.

Last night had been wonderful. I couldn't have imagined anything better, and she evidently thought the same. So why was she being so hateful about this weekend? Surely she realized I had to keep my gallery walls filled! How else could I sell paintings? Anyway, did we have to go to the camp to make love? We seemed to be doing okay on my mattress upstairs.

I began to feel anger, a sense of indignation. I finished the background in front of me and, yawning, began filling in another sky. I would try to complete as many swamp scenes as I could even if I had to hang them still dripping on the gallery walls.

It was afternoon and I was watching an old man feed one peanut at a time to a flock of pigeons. He opened each nut carefully and dropped the empty shells at his feet. The ground was littered, and I knew he was going to crumble the paper sack and drop that, too. He had just accomplished this amazing feat of littering when Ellen called.

"You were surprised that I called last night, weren't you?"

"Yes," I answered.

"Well, I was lying there in the dark making love to you."

I couldn't resist. Drawing in a deep breath, I said, "Ellen, you don't have to have sex with an imaginary me. We're both free. Why couldn't we have been together?" I do not ordinarily say things like that. Maybe because it had been after four o'clock when I'd cleaned my brushes and washed for bed and, after only an hour and a half of sleep, I was tired and irritable.

I watched the old man get to his feet and brush peanut shells from his lap to the ground. He walked away, scattering pigeons in all directions.

Ellen hadn't said anything, so I asked, "Are you still there?"

"I'm here." Her voice was flat, no emotion of any kind.

"I was just surprised when you called last night, that's all."

"Millie, I thought you'd like to know that I think about you when we're not together. It's not important to you, but I didn't know that when I called."

"Ellen, being with you is the most important thing in my life. That's why I want to be with you more than we are." I was whining again. I could hear it plain as day.

"You certainly don't show it. I wanted to please you, and you throw it back in my face."

Throw it back? Had I done that? She'd simply called to tell me I was in her thoughts. Obviously, I'm the one at fault.

"Ellen, I'm sorry. Honest, honey."

"What about this weekend? Are we going or not?"

"Sure we're going. And I have news for you about our suitcase ladies. Come tomorrow night, and I'll tell you what we've found out." Also, I thought, you'll have a real, live person in your arms.

"I don't know if I can. There's a meeting at the school that may run late, but I'll see." Her voice was brisk and impersonal.

"Will you call me tomorrow?"

She sighed loudly enough for me to hear. "Of course," she said.

I put the phone back on its shelf and started watching sparrows peck through the peanut debris.

Chapter 9

"Sister will be here this afternoon because I have my beauty appointment at two." Miss Leona touched her thinning blue hair and handed me a small purse. I'd had a last-minute portrait, so I was on the square later than usual. Miss Leona had kept my money overnight as she'd done many times.

"You did okay," I said, emptying two checks, three twenties, and some change on the kitchen table.

Miss Leona smiled, saying, "The cash is for your pastel rendering of the Cathedral and the Presbytère, and I sold a swamp scene and the riverboat race."

She was pleased because the boat race had been her idea. Paddle wheeler races on the Mississippi were complicated and took much longer than other paintings. They also sold for a lot more.

"Then I'd better get back to boat building, don't you think?"

Miss Leona beamed. Because of the price, the painting had hung longer than most. It was also larger than the sofa-size paintings that were popular. I was very pleased. The money would go to Lou, of course, and would help lower my debt to her father's firm. It also left a huge blank space on the wall.

"Your walls are almost empty, dear. Are you painting?"

I stared at my empty coffee cup. No, Miss Leona, I thought, I am not painting, and my walls are empty because I would rather be on the coast and in bed with Ellen.

"I started last night. Somehow I got a little behind," I explained.

She patted my hand. "You're a very good artist, my dear. Sister and I love your work."

"You know how much I appreciate what you do for me, don't you?"

She patted my hand again. "Sister and I enjoy helping."

At noon I sat on a bench in the square and ate half a roast beef po-boy from the grocery. It had been at least twelve inches long and loaded with meat, mayo, shredded lettuce, and tomatoes. I missed Micah already. I hadn't shared my lunch with him every day because he hadn't shown up on a daily basis, but he would have enjoyed eating the remaining half. He said he'd never heard of a po-boy anyplace but New Orleans.

I wrapped what was left, put it and my empty milk carton in the paper sack, and stood.

"Are you going to throw that away?"

A woman was standing at my side. She was huge, ugly, and had a small child in her arms. Her eyes were positively alight with eagerness. She was smiling, nodding her head, willing my answer to be yes.

"I didn't plan to," I answered, turning to face her.

"Oh," she said, disappointment clear. The child hadn't taken (his/her?) eyes off my face.

"But, if you'd like to have it, it's okay," I said.

"Please." She smiled, nodding again.

I put the bag in her outstretched hand and handed her a dollar. "For milk," I said.

The homeless have become a problem in the French Quarter, and particularly in the square, because they've set up living space on and around all of the benches and under every tree. They litter the ground with trash even though there are trash containers all over the place. Having no sanitary facilities, they've peed and squatted wherever they felt the need.

I can understand why they aren't wanted lounging and panhandling around New Orleans's most famous landmark. They seldom beg from the artists set up around the square, but they do approach tourists. Occasionally one will wander into my shop, hoping for a handout.

There was no way for me to know if the woman was a permanent squatter or if she'd just wandered in hoping to hit on someone. Whatever her problem, I felt sad seeing someone reduced to eating throw-away food.

After I left the square, not wanting to waste time eating out, I opened a can of chili for supper. When I sat at the table, my foot bumped the suitcase, which made me think of Marléne and Helen. The cemetery where Marléne was buried was a long streetcar ride down Canal Street, then many blocks to the cemetery gates. I'd wait until someone could drive me there. I'd leave my number with the custodian and hope the woman would call next time she brought flowers.

As I painted, my thoughts constantly turned to Ellen. Was she going to call? Just in case she did more than call, I closed the blinds.

After eight I heard a knock. We had a special signal that told me it was Ellen, and I almost fell off the chair in my haste to get to the door.

"Am I interrupting?" she asked as I pushed the door shut and snapped the lock. "You're working; I can smell the paint."

"No, no," I said. "I was just waiting for your call. Having you here is better." My arms hugged her waist, and I pulled her to me so that we could kiss.

"You know I can't keep my hands off, don't you?" I guided her to the love seat.

"Millie, we have to talk," she said, pushing me away.

"Can't we talk later?" I reached for her again.

"No, Millie, we have to get something straight."

"Okay," I said. "What?" I stood with my hands at

my side, not moving at all, waiting for what was to come.

"I want you to stop pressuring me about staying overnight. You know I have to be home because of Mother, but you keep nagging anyway. I want it to stop." She wasn't kidding, there was an underlying threat to her words.

Is this the same patient soul who said she avoided quarrels and confrontations, and who always kept things peaceful? I didn't think so. Stop, she'd said, or else what? I rose to the occasion.

"There's something here that I don't understand, Ellen. You won't go anyplace with me except to the camp. You come here in the dead of night and leave before morning, and we never go anyplace where people might see us. Are you ashamed of me?" I know I'm not a cover girl but neither am I too ugly to be seen in public.

Ellen's eyes narrowed, and my question went unanswered. "This is just how it is, Millie." She gritted her teeth. "I didn't plan to become a fixture around here, and if that's what you expected, then you totally misunderstood." She stepped closer, for emphasis, I guess.

I think my mouth dropped level with my knees. I could see any future with Ellen gurgling down the drain. "Please," I said. "Please. I didn't expect anything like that at all." An out-and-out lie.

"Well, it certainly sounded like it." Her tone was slightly conciliatory, and I took heart.

I touched her arm, and she didn't draw back. "Let me ask you one thing?" This was what had puzzled me, and I had to ask even at the risk of blowing everything. "When we first got together, sex was wonderful. But then you began to act like you didn't want any." I saw her lips forming a smile, so I rushed on. "Now you want it again. Is it something I'm doing?" I fervently hoped so.

Ellen snorted. Then she actually smiled. "Millie, everything you do in bed is fine. I told you that finding the suitcase turned me on sexually, and it still does." Now she moved closer. I could feel her breath on my face. "I came here tonight for some loving. I don't want to quarrel. I just needed to get things straight between us." Cupping my face in her hands, she guided my mouth to hers.

No quarrel, I thought? As always, she had made her boundaries crystal clear before I could get my mouth open. We don't go out in public. I'm not to ask for more than she intends to give. We meet only to have sex, and now her turn-on is a suitcase full of old clothes. Take it or leave it.

As her mouth sucked me in, I had a vision of my loft draped with Marléne's dresses. They hung so low over the bed that I could feel the soft fabric caressing my back as Ellen's open thighs invited my touch.

After Ellen left I started painting again, but my mind was full of the questions I had never asked. I thought of how little I really knew about her except that she lived with her mother out near the lake and that she taught school.

I figured that she was ashamed of being with me

and felt that she needed to hide our relationship. She probably felt it necessary to keep up a straight appearance because of work and her mother. That was understandable. I knew couples who had hidden their loving relationship for years because of family.

Ellen was only going to see me when she felt safe, and I crossed my fingers that someday that would change. If I wanted her in my bed, I had to accept her terms. And I wanted her in my bed! More and more I wanted her in my bed and in my life.

I'd had affairs with several women for various periods of time. The affairs were mostly casual on my part and mostly for sex. I had never considered even one of them as a lifelong partner, nor had I ever moved in with anyone. I enjoyed my freedom. As shy as I am, I managed an occasional one-night stand, but I had never been as sexually motivated as I was with Ellen.

I was painting gray moss on oak limbs when I decided to keep my mouth shut and live with the arrangement we had. No nagging, no pressure. I was putting in the watery reflections of a tiny cabin with a light in one window when I decided to ask Lou for a ride to the cemetery. As I was signing my name and the date, I decided to ask Lou not to come to the camp on the weekend. I was cleaning my brushes when I decided to unearth my dildo and take it to Mississippi. I didn't need it, but maybe Ellen would find it enjoyable.

The phone rang at least ten times before I could

pry myself off the bed. "I knew you were home," Lou said. "Hope I didn't interrupt anything."

"Naw," I said before a huge yawn almost dislocated my jaw. "I was just resting . . . alone."

"Are we going to the camp tomorrow?"

"Yes and no, Lou. Ellen and I are but I, ah, want to be alone with her, understand?" At least, I hoped Ellen was going. We hadn't discussed it, being too busy for conversation.

"Sure, I understand."

"Would you do me a favor? Drive me to the cemetery next week so I can talk with the custodian?"

"Yep. When do you want to go?" Talking to the custodian had been Lou's idea in the first place.

"Doesn't matter," I said. "Whenever you're free."

"I'll call you Monday. Y'all have fun, hear?"

How thankful I was to have Lou for a friend. I wondered about Peaches. I should have asked, I thought, because Lou was certainly suffering. I hoped Peaches had stayed in Mississippi.

Ellen called a few minutes later. "I'll pick you up at your door in the morning at eight sharp. And, Millie, would it upset you if I told you how much I enjoyed tonight?"

"What did you enjoy about it?" I asked softly.

"You know what I enjoy. It makes me blush to think about it."

"Come back and I'll do it again." Asking her to come back was a generic statement designed to let her know I'd like a repeat performance, too. I hoped she'd take it that way because I certainly wasn't trying to pressure her.

"Darling, I would if I could. Can you hold that thought until tomorrow?"

"I'll have a surprise for you tomorrow, something you may enjoy even more." I was thinking about my dildo.

"I can't imagine anything better. What if we spent some time at your place before we head for the coast? I'm like Helen. I don't like to wait, either."

"I don't think Miss Leona would enjoy hearing us carry on over her head, but we could stop in a motel on the way, you know." The sexual innuendos were making me horny, and a motel was beginning to sound like a good idea. If the only thing between us was going to be sex, then I'd see that we had enough to keep us both satisfied. We'd have quantity and all the variations I could think of.

Chapter 10

Ellen was quiet on the drive to the coast. When we pulled into the driveway she turned to me as I was opening my door.

"I have to go back this evening, Millie. I can't stay until Sunday." She touched my arm with her fingertips, pressing to hold me in place.

I felt disappointment, certainly, but a tiny flash of anger, too. I stared at her, not speaking.

"I'm sorry, this is something at school that just came up, a Sunday morning parent conference that I didn't know about."

"Why didn't you tell me last night?" I would have asked Lou to come this evening. and we'd have worked tonight and Sunday. I was already taking off the most profitable times on the square to be here finishing the interior. Now no work would get done this weekend.

Ellen shrugged. "Do you want to stay? We could go back to New Orleans right now if you like." She sounded like it didn't matter one way or the other.

"If I like? Seems to me it's what you like," I barked. Turning away I looked across my weedy yard at the Gulf. Taking a deep breath didn't help.

"Let's go," I said, slamming my door shut. So much for the great dildo surprise.

Gravel flying, we screeched to the interstate and, going well over the speed limit, set a record time for the ride back.

I worked on the square the rest of Saturday and all day Sunday. Monday Lou called before I got my cart out the door. We ate at a waffle place, neither of us cheerful, and Lou was sensitive enough not to ask why my lip was poking out.

The cemetery custodian was riding a slow-moving machine that made a lot of noise but didn't seem to cut anything. He was friendly enough, especially after I handed him a twenty.

"I don't know if I see her every time she comes," he explained. "I'm working all around here, you know."

"If you do see her, you'll give her this, won't you?" I handed him a card with both my numbers and a note that gave her the reason I wanted to make contact. All perfectly straightforward.

"Just keep your fingers crossed," Lou advised when she slowed in front of my gallery to let me out of the car. Miss Leona was inside.

"Any calls for me?" I asked.

"No, dear, but I have some money for you."

"I'll collect this evening," I said, pushing the cart out the door.

Weekly and on weekends I worked the square for the next month. At night I painted, not only filling the gallery walls but managing to complete so many swamp scenes that I had to store them in the loft.

Lou met me some mornings, and we'd go across the street for coffee and beignets. Frank hadn't reappeared, and no one at the coffee shop knew why. Knowing his frantic lifestyle, I told Lou he was probably on cloud nine with a new lover. "He'll show up someday," I predicted.

Miss Leona had news for me. "Sister and I are going to Mamou for our family reunion next Saturday, and we plan to stay until Tuesday." The reunion was a yearly summer affair that the sisters enjoyed. They brought back photos of their newest nieces and nephews, round-faced babies, all of whom looked alike, squinting into the sun. I could either sit the gallery or close it and work the square.

For the first time, the square was beginning to make me itch. I was deadly tired of watching tourists take pictures of the Cabildo, the Cathedral, the Presbytère and me. In my sleep I could hear the click of camera shutters and feel my eyes go temporarily blind from unexpected flashes of light aimed directly at my face. It was time I took a few days off from the square. I would sit in my shop, turn the air up and the stereo on, and wait for people to pay me for what I love to do.

When the phone rang I'd jump for it, but it was either unimportant or it was Lou. I'm pretty much of a loner, so I didn't expect a lot of calls. Lou and I ate together a couple of times a week, but I was as depressed as Lou. We mostly stared across the table at each other.

"Did Peaches ever get here from Mississippi?" I asked one evening just to make conversation. I watched Lou frown, add sugar to her tea, stare past my head, and finally settle on her plate as the most interesting object in the room.

"Yeah, Millie." Nothing more, just "Yeah, Millie."

"I should have asked sooner, Lou," I said. "I knew how important it was to you."

"That's okay. It's over, finished and forgotten." She was lying in her teeth.

"Then why are you still in the dump? You're sure it's over?"

"It's over as far as I'm concerned, but Peaches keeps pestering me. She calls and cries like a baby, and I don't know what to do. There's really no point to calling because I'm through with her. She just doesn't want to believe it. She says she can cause a lot of trouble if she wants."

"What kind of trouble?" Lou was pretty out about her lifestyle, and her father was her employer. What trouble could Peaches mean? Sudden suspicion made me add, "Does she want money?"

Lou was nodding, her interest again on her plate. She studied the remains of her eggplant Parmesan before lifting her gaze to meet mine. "Money?" she questioned, adding, "I guess that's what she always wanted. She didn't want me, that's for sure." That had to have been a devastating blow to Lou's ego. I knew, because the person I loved didn't want me, either, and I was numb with pain.

"We're twins, Lou. Ellen and I have broken up for about the same reason, except that Ellen didn't want money. She just didn't want me." There! I said it aloud and the roof didn't fall in.

"I guessed it was like that. It didn't take a crystal ball to see that something happened. I wanted to help, but I didn't know what to do there either." Lou's concern was genuine. In a gesture totally unlike her, she reached across the table and covered my hand with hers. "It'll be okay, Millie. You'll find someone else."

"Don't want anyone else." That was true as of that minute, but when you've had great sex on a regular basis it's hard to do without, especially when it isn't your decision. I'd fantasized, using my own hands to do what Ellen used to do, and I got results, but there was no feeling of deep satisfaction that you share with a partner. Sex with yourself, I've decided, is for the birds. What I desired most was Ellen.

Lou had something else on her mind. She fiddled with her napkin, making deep creases as she folded and refolded it. She said, "I think I've found someone."

"Wonderful," I exclaimed. "Who?"

"She works at the pipe supply place, and I've known her for a while. We've done business now and then for about a year." Lou leaned forward and lowered her voice. "She told me she was gay. Not in so many words, mind you, but I knew that's what she meant. Right now she's living at home, but she wants to move out, she says. I asked her to have supper with me Saturday, and she said she'd like to."

Dear God, I thought, please let this woman be gay. Lou sometimes heard what she wanted to hear, not what was actually said.

"I know you'll have a wonderful time, Lou. What's her name?"

"Bonnye, with a *Y*. I saw it on her name tag and asked her about the spelling. She said it was a family name. I told her my name was actually Louella but that I hadn't been called that since first grade."

"I didn't know you were a Louella. You never told me."

"I never told anybody. Listen, Millie, if we don't end up at the movies Saturday night, could we come by your place? I explained to Bonnye that you were my best friend, and she'd like to meet you . . . if you're not busy, that is."

"One thing's for sure, I won't be busy. I'd like to meet her, so y'all come on over." I wasn't busy any night, I thought, so I'd get a chance to check out Lou's newest.

I had fallen asleep in front of the TV, which wasn't strange because I was watching it from my bed. Raspy lines accompanied a crackle on the screen, so before I answered the phone I pushed the Off button.

"Hello." There was no answer. No heavy breathing, either. I was about to hang up when I heard, "Millie?" It was Ellen. I jerked to a sitting position. "Ellen?"

"Yes," she said, "it's Ellen."

I was speechless for a dozen heartbeats. "Where are you?" Foolish question, but my brain had shut down.

"I'm in my car outside your door."

It took another dozen heartbeats for this to register. "Outside my door?"

"Wake up, Millie. Yes, I'm parked just opposite your door. Will you come down and let me in?"

My bare toes scraped painfully on the iron steps, but I didn't stop. I didn't even move the blind aside to make sure it was Ellen; I just snapped the lock and pulled open the door. It was Ellen. I stepped aside then pushed the door closed after her. She walked a few steps into the room and turned to face me. The blinds were up, so I could see her face. "Yes, Millie," she said quietly, "I've wanted you, too."

My arms, her arms: who reached for the other first? We clung, bodies pressed close, mouths open, tongues tasting. I pulled her tighter to me, my hands firm on her buttocks. After a moment I realized she was wearing something long and silky. I took my mouth from hers and looked. She was wearing a gown and robe, neither concealing the hardness of her nipples.

Our breathing could have been heard all the way to Canal Street. I touched her breasts, my fingers caressing the hardness, and I heard her breath catch. "You've wanted me too?" It was a statement, really, not a question at all.

Her answer was clear. She took my face between her hands and guided my lips to hers again. Except for my entire body being ablaze, I could have stayed there in my gallery, in front of a glass display window, kissing all night. She moved from me finally and, taking my hand, led me to the stairs.

The brightness of a full moon showed her face. She was naked, the gown and robe lost somewhere in the tangle of bedclothes. We had made love frantically at first, then a little more slowly, and then again with an urgency that surprised both of us, I think. It was very late, and I waited for her to head for the shower. She didn't move except to turn on her side. Her mouth close to my ear, she whispered, "It's getting light, my darling."

I was surprised when her hand began exploring. She raised on an elbow and began tasting my breast with her tongue. "Shall I continue?" she asked. My body answered for me.

Another hour and it was dawn. The sun was up and the skylight showed clear blue heaven. "Don't you have to go?" I was afraid she had stayed too late.

"No, I do not have to go. Call your Miss Leona and tell her not to come today because you're not well and have decided to close the shop. You and I are going to spend the whole day doing you-know-what, and we don't want to be disturbed."

I did just that. We did spend time doing you-know-what, but we also showered and I got Ellen's clothes out of her car trunk so that she wouldn't have to walk to a restaurant in her nightgown. Later we managed to get to the coffee shop.

We didn't talk about the last month. I didn't ask why she could stay overnight with me, and she didn't offer any explanation for not going to her job on a weekday. What we did was walk close together in public, so close that I felt we were almost holding hands.

Late in the afternoon we looked through the suitcase again, and I told Ellen about the card and note I'd left at the cemetery. "Do you think we'll ever hear anything?" She was examining the snapshot, holding it up to the light.

"Maybe," I said, "maybe not. Who knows?"

Ellen sat back in her chair. "Darling, I have to go now."

We had been getting close to this moment all day, so I was ready. "Okay. Will you call me when you get some free time?" I didn't think that was too much to ask. After all, I wasn't nagging, just asking a simple question.

"Of course I will." She leaned and gave me a gentle kiss. "Was a whole night together under your skylight as good as you expected?" Ha! I had bitched and bitched about us spending a weeknight together, and she had come to me in her nightgown, prepared to do just that!

I could say it now. I took both of her hands in mine. "I'm in love with you, Ellen." She didn't look startled or even surprised.

"I love you, too, Millie. I've known it for a long time."

How simple! We loved each other. What more was there to say? I didn't give a damn who was watching,

I held her hand as we crossed the sidewalk to her car. She didn't seem to care.

Her nightgown and robe were still upstairs on the bed. I untangled them from the disaster we had made of the sheets and went to sleep that night with their silken softness cradled in my arms.

Chapter 11

Ellen was a classy lady. I don't think I will ever forget how quickly she made Bonnye feel at ease Saturday night when Bonnye and Lou stopped by the gallery. I had told Ellen that we might have company, so we stayed out of bed — a hardship, considering how much we wanted to be in it.

Ellen walked around the corner to the grocery and came back with a sack full of nibbly things, some wine, cola, and toothpicks with little cellophane hats. I was cleaning the kitchen floor and trying to decide if I could paint it some nice neutral color and have time for it to dry before our company arrived . . . if they came, that is.

I was pleased that Ellen had gone out in broad daylight and that it had been her idea to get munchies and something other than water to drink.

"What were you going to offer them?" she asked, putting the drinks in my empty fridge. "You have five greasy sandwich parts and a pound of rancid butter. Did you think that would be enough?"

"I didn't think about it at all. Lou doesn't expect me to feed her."

"Perhaps not, but you do want Bonnye to think you're civilized, don't you?" Ellen turned back to the fridge in pretended exasperation. We had stayed in town because of Lou. We spent the day walking in the Quarter like tourists and had lunched at one of those fancy places where you pay a fortune for one bite of food that's usually not recognizable except for the description in the menu, and then only if you speak French.

As we walked, looking in windows, we had touched arms and shoulders and brushed hands to the point that I stayed somewhere between simple arousal and throwing Ellen to the ground.

To me, the touching was foreplay even if we were in public. Finally Ellen grabbed my arm and hissed, "If you scrape against me one more time I'm leaving!"

"Leaving?" I squeaked.

"Yes, leaving! You will simply have to tell Miss Leona to go home, that we'll watch the shop. Understand?"

I stumbled for words. To my great delight, I finally said, "Oh."

To get there faster, we took a cab. To get rid of Miss Leona, I told a horrendous lie. To keep people away from my door, I hung the Closed sign and shut the blinds.

Bonnye was more or less what I expected. More, because she was truly beautiful, and less, because at first I didn't think she was gay. Lou was smitten. Here we go again, I thought, as Lou made the introductions. Bonnye had good manners, auburn hair, brown eyes, and was seemingly fascinated by my paintings. I noticed her stealing glances around the walls when there was a lull in the conversation.

"Would you like to look at any particular one?" I finally asked. Lou stood by her side, munching cheese and crackers, and smiling fatuously.

One painting of colored wildflowers in the yard of a bayou cabin seemed to attract her. "The wind's blowing, isn't it?" She pointed at the faint ripples in the water and the flowers nodding toward the house.

"Yes, it's a gentle breeze, but it does seem to make the flowers dance. Most people don't see that, I'm afraid."

"Well, if that's the one you want, it's yours!" Lou reached for her wallet.

Bonnye smiled shyly at me and nodded. "Yes, that's the one."

"Hold it!" I said to Lou, my hand on her arm. "If it's for you there's no charge; you know that."

"No," Lou said, "I want to buy it for Bonnye. That makes it different." She opened her wallet, squinted at the price tag on the painting, and started counting bills.

"I'm not going to take your money, Lou," I said firmly, shaking my head for emphasis.

Lou grunted and, with a sheepish grin, replaced the money in her wallet. The interchange wasn't lost on Bonnye, and I think Lou gained stature in Bonnye's eyes because of it.

It was Lou who began talking about the camp. "Y'all going next weekend?" she asked.

Ellen and I looked at each other. Were we going? At Ellen's barely perceptible shrug I said, "Don't know yet but probably. We'll decide later in the week, right Ellen?"

I took down the painting and wrapped it. During the general conversation that followed I decided that I liked Bonnye, that Bonnye was gay after all, and that she was getting a crush on Lou in a big way. That pleased me.

When they were gone Ellen began putting away the snacks that were left. "Ellen," I said, "leave those crumbs for the mice, please. We have other, more important things to do."

Ellen turned to me, all innocence, and asked, "We do? What, pray tell?"

I whispered in her ear exactly what we were going to do. I added that this was only our second Saturday night there and that we should make the most of it. To our credit, we had been circumspect the entire evening, a great accomplishment considering that we hadn't touched each other since early afternoon.

She was very slow taking off her clothes. I had shed everything in seconds and now waited, watching. I expected her to fall naked into my arms, but she took her robe off the hanger and pulled it over her head.

I could see her nipples straining against the fabric.

"Put your hands under my gown, Millie. I saw how that excited you the other night."

That was the understatement of the year, but I let it pass without comment. I was occupied doing as she asked.

Ellen picked me up at my door Wednesday evening, and we went to a movie at one of the old neighborhood theaters that shows film classics and oddball features. They were trying to hang on, but there were only six other paying customers tonight. Their future looked bleak from where we sat on the back row, but we were able to take advantage of their misfortune by holding hands and stealing an occasional daring peck on the cheek. As best I remember, it was about a prisoner of war bouncing a ball against the wall of his cell. It was in color, too . . . I think.

Why go to a movie? No reason, except that it's the kind of thing real people do. We didn't stay to see the end.

On our way back to the Quarter, we passed the cemetery where Marléne was buried. "You haven't heard anything?" Ellen asked, her attention on the Canal Street traffic turning into Metairie Road.

"Wish I had," I said, admiring the competent way she handled the car. I know how to drive but, after four years of buses, streetcars, and feet, I wasn't very practiced.

"Ellen, tell me what would have happened if you'd been stopped the other night? Whatever gave you the nerve to drive through town in your nightgown?"

"You already know the answer to that, my darling. I was heartsick and missing you to the point that I couldn't sleep for thinking about us. I was in bed when it struck me that being with you was the only thing that could make me happy, and that you weren't asking the impossible. A whole night together sounded like heaven to me, too, so I took the chance that you'd be home and that you'd want to see me."

"What if you hadn't found a parking place outside my door?"

"I would have simply walked to your door in my nightgown. This is New Orleans, you know. No one would have noticed."

"Don't ever get rid of that gown," I warned.

I washed my clothes at the laundry place a couple of blocks down Ursulines Avenue, and I had left the basket, with gown and robe inside, on a kitchen chair. Miss Leona had kindly folded the lot for me. I wondered what she thought about such feminine delicacies in with my jeans and work shirts and strictly utilitarian underwear.

110

We did go to the camp the next weekend. Once we had lugged food and clothes upstairs, Ellen and I opened all the windows so the place could air. We were changing the sheets in our bedroom when Lou and Bonnye arrived. They had brought food, too, and four steaks the size of the Superdome. I was trying to fit the meat in my refrigerator freezer when Lou came up behind me.

"Uh, Millie," she said leaning over my ear. "We're not gonna stay overnight. I mean, we'll stay but at a motel. Understand?"

I certainly did understand. "Sure, Lou," I said.

"We may not be here early enough for breakfast, either."

"No problem. Ellen and I'll get started, and you can pitch in when you get here." It was hard for me to wipe the grin off my face, but I turned to her and said, "Y'all enjoy, okay?"

Lou was beet red. As close as we'd been over the years, we had not spoken openly about our lesbianism. Not until recently, that is.

Work was the order of the day, and we did just that. Bonnye knew how to swing a hammer and finish Sheetrock, so she pitched in, doing whatever we asked, and by evening our kitchen had walls on all four sides. After they left, Ellen and I stood in the doorway to admire our handiwork.

"Remember Peaches?" Ellen asked. "She never lifted a finger except to apply polish. I don't know what Lou ever saw in her, do you?"

"I don't think Lou was attracted to her because she could do carpenter work. There were probably other reasons, hon."

"I guess so." Ellen turned to me. "Lou took Bonnye to a motel for a reason, so I hope Bonnye knows what's expected of her."

"They've probably worked it out. Lou isn't the type to force herself on anyone."

"Like me?" Ellen's expression, guileless and totally innocent, made me burst into laughter.

"Come," I said, turning her to face the bedroom, "I think I'll let you force yourself on me."

Sunday at noon we lit the grill and sat on the balcony waiting for the coals to get just right for steak. Lou was playing chef and, from what I could tell, their evening had been one to remember. Bonnye watched Lou's every move, a Mona Lisa smile on her face. And Lou? What can I say? The steaks were raw on one side and crispy black on the other. We ate anyway.

On our way back across the Twin Spans Sunday night I kept my hand on Ellen's thigh. We rode in blissful silence, listening to soft music from the car radio. I jerked to attention when Ellen said, "Darling, I have something to tell you."

We were too recently together for me not to be afraid. My heart thudding because I didn't know what was coming, I said bravely, "If it's bad news, don't tell me, okay?"

"Depends on how you look at it," Ellen said evasively, glancing at me before giving her attention to the bridge traffic again.

I crossed my arms and took a deep breath. "Okay," I said. "I'm ready. What is it?"

"It's semester break, and I can stay with you Tuesday, Wednesday, and Thursday, if you like, my darling." She was smiling at me, nothing like Mona

Lisa. It was a happy smile, reflecting her pleasure in giving me a surprise that answered my dreams.

Tuesday, Wednesday, Thursday . . . it was a good thing my gallery was full of paintings and more in the loft. Miss Leona kept the gallery open and kept money coming in because I certainly wasn't doing anything to earn dollars. Ellen and I became tourists.

We went to the museum and the zoo. We picnicked on the levy. We rode the Saint Charles streetcar, our arms touching. One entire day, from early to late, we toured the old mansions along River Road and crossed the river for Oak Alley.

We made love at night after Miss Leona left. After our sexual excitement peaked, we held each other, satisfied, our bodies close and warm, breathing in soft kisses, drifting slowly into sleep.

Had I once believed Ellen only wanted me because I satisfied her in bed? Could I have believed anything so obviously stupid? We were together now, heart to heart, and I loved her more each day that passed.

Thursday night being the last, we celebrated by having dinner at an expensive restaurant. Ellen wore a dress that caused my breath to catch and high heels that brought us exactly eye to eye. I wore slacks because it was all I had.

We lingered over the meal. It was late when we finished our coffee and too far to walk back to the gallery, so I hailed a passing cab. It wasn't one of the cab companies I knew, but it looked clean. "Where to, girls?" the driver asked.

I gave him the address and settled back next to Ellen.

The distance was only a few blocks, so the ride was short. The driver didn't open the door for us,

113

but none of them ever does. I handed him what he asked for and a dollar tip. As I was turning away I heard him snicker. "You dykes sure you don't want me to take you to the Golden Dove?"

I stiffened, then whirled to look at him. His teeth were bared in a lecherous grin, his left arm hanging outside the door and the middle finger of his left hand making poking motions at me. I could feel my head explode. Without thought I darted across the walk, grabbed his arm, and twisted. He howled, jerked his arm back and, slamming the car into motion, roared away. I stood there, my heart racing, taking huge breaths in an effort to get calm.

Ellen, her face showing both concern and fright, asked, "What happened, Millie? What was that all about?"

My voice was shaking when I answered. "Did you hear what he said?"

"Something about a dove?" We were standing in my doorway, Ellen's arms tight around me.

"Called us dykes, said we belonged at the Golden Dove. It's a raunchy lesbian bar in the ninth ward. I've only heard what goes on there but, believe me, you wouldn't want to be caught dead anyplace near it." I was calmer, so I fitted my key in the lock and we went inside.

"Why would he say that? I don't understand."

So discouraged I was near tears, I said, "I don't know why. It's just what some people do. The bastard!"

Ellen cocked her head, narrowed her eyes. "He could tell we were lesbians. Is that what upset you?"

"I guess so." The tears began to stream. I wiped

my cheeks with my hand. "Ellen, I'm so sorry," I began.

"Sweetheart, don't let that asshole get the best of you. We are who we are. I'm not ashamed of loving you."

Now I was sobbing. "I didn't want anything like that to happen to you." It was anger and a feeling of helplessness that caused my tears.

"Stop crying, my darling. It's over, finished." She led me to the stairs and we climbed to the loft but, for me, our special evening had been soiled.

Chapter 12

Every major hotel in New Orleans had a convention, so the Quarter was flooded with tourists. Most of the people were dressed in ordinary clothes and comfortable shoes and flashed their cameras every two minutes. Others wore identical hats or vests or carried some symbol that enabled them to recognize one another in passing.

It was a noisy weekend on the square, and at times I actually had people standing in line. After a while, they all began to have the same features. Depicting them as special individuals took concentration. I spent many minutes staring at perfect strangers posing in front of me, trying to pick whatever it was that made them unique so that I could include it in their portrait.

By afternoon my cash box was overflowing, and I was starving. Having nothing but soft drinks all day tended to make me growl. I could have taken a few minutes for lunch, but I hated to miss a sale.

The shadows were lengthening, but still tourists crowded the streets. By then my smile was fixed and I kept conversation to a minimum while doing my best to give the customers their money's worth. Moving back from the easel to stretch aching shoulders, I saw Frank hovering near my cart. I was concerned that something bad had happened, so I was pleased to see him.

"Hi, Millie," he said, waving his fingers and grinning sheepishly.

The phrase "our eyes met" flashed through my head, but that's exactly what took place. Our eyes did meet and I said, "Hi, Frank. Where've you been all this time?"

He sidled closer, his grin wider. "Oh, I've been here and there."

I studied his face. He's ill, I thought. Very little color was in his cheeks, and a tinge of gray under his eyes made him look fragile. "Well," I said, "I'm glad you're back from wherever you went. Did you have a good time?"

He rolled his eyes. "It was perfectly lovely, Millie. I wouldn't have missed it for anything!" His generic kind of answer, so different from the Frank I knew, made it clear he didn't intend to give me chapter and verse of his odyssey to that perfectly lovely place. I figured the place must have been less than perfect and perhaps not very lovely at all.

"Ya hungry?" I asked.

"Something to eat would be nice," he said primly.

I looked around, didn't see anyone who looked like an immediate customer, so I hauled my bulging cash box out of the cart and closed the doors. "Going for something to eat," I told my artist neighbor. "I'll be back in a few minutes."

It wasn't a restaurant-type restaurant, but it was more than a hot dog stand. There were tables, food prices printed on a mirror behind the serving counter, vats of salad, a steam table with mostly hot dogs, and a bored young man to collect the money . . . hot dog, chili, and a Coke for me, a bun and potato salad for Frank.

As I added hot mustard to my dog, I said, "Thought you were hungry, Frank. It's my treat, so eat up."

"I had a huge lunch, so this little bit is all I want."

We sat at an outside table, both watching the passing crowd. I wolfed down my dog, went back for more chili, and saw that Frank had barely touched his plate.

"Is something wrong?" I asked after my last bite.

His eyes were huge, and they filled with tears as he struggled for an answer. "I have AIDS," he said simply.

"No." I shook my head. "Ah, no."

He nodded, not speaking. Finally he took in a deep breath, folded his hands on the table, and said, "I have no money, no place to stay, no insurance, no nothing." He shrugged. "They won't take me back at the Café du Monde, and I don't know how to do anything except wait tables, Millie."

We stared at each other. Frank expected something of me, I could tell by his expression. Trying to put off what was surely coming I asked, already knowing the answer, "What happened to your new lover?"

"Gone. He left when I told him."

"Your family?" Surely there was someone to care.

"They won't have anything to do with me. They put me out."

Frank and I had never been friends in the true sense of the word, only two people who spoke casually once in a while. This flashed through my mind at the same time my mouth opened to speak. "What can I do to help?" I asked. It would have been more than cruel to make him beg, although that's what he had come prepared to do.

"If you could lend me enough to get a place to stay for a few days, there are people who'll help me. I'll pay you back," he promised.

My bulging cash box was next to my plate. "Sure, I'll lend you a few bucks. You have to pay me back, you know, when you get settled and find a job." We both knew I'd never see a cent of whatever I handed him. Why did I feel it necessary to pretend that everything was going to be okay some day?

"Count on it, Millie." His attention now on the cash box, he sat forward in his chair, waiting.

I opened the box, fumbled with a pile of bills, counted out two hundred, and handed it to him. Was it enough? Too much? I had no way of knowing. Four years in the Quarter, four years of saying no to beggars, had eliminated any charitable impulses I may have had at one time. Perhaps word got around. I can't say, but I was seldom approached any more, either on the square or in my gallery.

Frank's eagerness to get away was apparent. I didn't care. I was impatient for him to go, too. He pocketed the cash, saying, "Thanks, Millie."

Waving him away with a smile, I took my last swallow of Coke and went back to my easel.

It was business as usual until four drunks, all huge and wearing cowboy hats, wanted a group portrait. I could have made back the two hundred I had given Frank, but I didn't feel like fooling with them. "Sorry, boys," I said. "I'm quitting for the day." I pointed to my neighbor who was watching. "He'll be happy to do your portrait."

After some grumbling and a few crude remarks, they staggered away. I packed my cart and wheeled it to the gallery. Miss Leona had a fistful of money for me, so we had instant coffee at the table and settled accounts. I was in the shower when, of course, the phone rang. Thinking it could be Ellen, I ran for it.

"Have you eaten yet?" Lou asked.

We walked to the spaghetti place and ordered from the same snotty waiter. "Millie, guess what?" Lou was so full of whatever it was that she leaned halfway across the table, saying in a whisper that shook the walls, "Bonnye is moving in with me! We talked it over a little while ago, and she's telling her parents now. Whatcha think about that?"

What did I think about that? We hadn't seen Lou very much lately, so Ellen and I figured she and Bonnye were courting and, knowing Lou as I did, it was reasonable to predict that they would soon live together. "That's really great, Lou!"

They were meant for each other, Lou explained, so living together would be right. Both wanted it that way.

I couldn't help the thoughts that crossed my mind as Lou rushed to tell me their plans. Who is paying for this upheaval, I wondered, and will you share expenses? Is Bonnye going to keep working as a clerk in the pipe company or will she sit home doing her nails as Peaches did?

My heart sank to ankle level. Lou saw the roses; I saw the thorns. "When we get settled, you and Ellen can come eat with us. Bonnye is a wonderful cook!"

"We'll look forward to it, Lou," I said.

"If you're going to the camp this weekend, we plan to head over there, too. Bonnye thinks the camp is fun. She wants to help finish it."

Well, score one for Bonnye, I thought. She's certainly a change from Peaches. "I'll let you know sometime this week, okay?"

Lou checked her watch and raced off to meet Bonnye. I walked home and settled in for the night with a book. I didn't expect Ellen to call because of some kind of seminar that night, tomorrow night, and Tuesday. It didn't cause a problem anymore because we were together more than I'd ever hoped. I had accepted Ellen's need to balance time with me and time with her mother so that there wasn't too much stress.

Ellen hadn't moved in with me, but it was only in bed that there was room enough for two anyway. I had furnished the gallery with a love seat, some chairs, and four occasional tables with two of my small, framed Quarter scenes displayed on each one.

It simply wasn't a cozy room for sitting and watching TV. It was strictly a gallery, and the walls were covered with paintings that I hoped to sell.

My painting room was next, only large enough for my easel, two file cabinets, and my painting supplies. The kitchen did have a three-burner stove, a small refrigerator, a table, and a sink with cabinets underneath. The toilet and shower were behind the kitchen stairway and the spiral steps led to my sleeping loft.

My quarters were large enough for one to live and work in comfort but were not suitable for two. I didn't even have a closet, just an armoire. Anyway, Ellen and I hadn't talked about living together. I think it was in the back of my mind, but it certainly wasn't in hers. I had lived alone for a long time and had grown accustomed to solitude. The thought of moving, even to be with Ellen, was more frightening than appealing.

Yawning, I put down my book, turned on the TV, and started thinking about Frank. The end was inevitable, of course, and I felt a deep sorrow. Frank had operated at the emotional level of a twelve-year-old, but he was friendly and kind and I liked him. The TV began fizzing, so I turned it off and stared at the evening sky until I fell asleep.

Ellen told me that we could go to the camp on Friday after work, so I was packed and waiting when she tooted. "Hi'ya, babe," I said, throwing my things in the backseat.

"Know what I want to do?" she asked as we climbed the interstate approach. We hadn't seen each other for six days, so I didn't have to guess. "You want to stop in Slidell at the new motel?" We had done this a few times just for the hell of it. It was nice to hop out of a bed that someone else was going to make, eat food someone else cooked, then get back on the road without having to do dishes.

"Well, yes and no. There's a barbecue hut next to the interstate that just opened, and I'd like to try it."

"That's the yes. What's the no?"

"I have to come home Saturday afternoon. There's just no getting out of it, Millie. You can't know how I tried."

Often Ellen would have to cut short our weekend, so I was grateful that we'd at least have that night. I'd call Lou from the motel to see if she and Bonnye were really coming. We were almost at the point of finishing all the rooms, thanks to Bonnye's skill in taping Sheetrock. Saturday nights she and Lou still checked into a motel, but that was fine with Ellen and me.

We ate barbecue, bathed together in the luxurious motel bath, and retired early. Ellen wrapped herself around me, her gown the only thing between us, and started whispering in my ear. "I'm wearing a gown, my darling. Don't you want to see what's underneath?" A rhetorical question, no doubt.

We stayed in bed almost until checkout time. Before we left I called Lou to make sure she'd be there so that I'd have a ride back to New Orleans on Sunday.

Ellen liked to paint with a roller, so she had become the official painter. I sanded the seams; Ellen came behind me and covered the walls with a light beige, not quite white, paint. We were making great progress by the time Lou and Bonnye pulled into the driveway.

The tiny hallway was the last to be tackled and, even with the four of us bumping into one another like crabs in a bucket, we managed to get it finished. Bonnye thought we should celebrate with the champagne they happened to have, so we opened the bottle and sat on the hall floor toasting the camp and one another.

In the afternoon, I walked Ellen down to her car. I was leaning in the driver's window to give her another kiss, there being no one around for miles, when she whispered, "I'll bet the champagne was for the two of them tonight."

"Yeah, they probably celebrate making love, that's what I think. Except that I don't particularly like to drink, we could have done that, too," I whispered back.

"Millie, you've got to be kidding! We would be bombed out of our minds nine-tenths of the time."

I snickered and nodded my head in agreement. Going back upstairs, I wondered how soon it would be before I saw her again.

Miss Leona always placed my mail on the kitchen table. Mostly it was composed of bills and advertisements, but there was a letter on university

124

stationery that didn't look like either. It was handwritten and it was from Micah.

He was back in the chemistry department, he wrote, and again doing work he loved. The break from his normal routines had given him a new perspective, he said, and he might do it again some day. Had I learned any more about Marléne and Helen? Would I please let him know? Another couple of lines then he signed it with affection.

I put the letter back in the envelope, pleased to have heard from him. It was good to know that he was happy. I tacked the letter to my easel for safe-keeping. Someday, maybe, I'd need the address if we learned more about Marléne and Helen.

Tuesday must have been school day because there were groups and groups of children, lined in rows, going from the Cabildo to the Cathedral to the Presbytère. I sat at my easel doing another sample for the fence. In addition to the portraits, I made pretty good money from my sketches of General Jackson and his horse. Sometimes I drew the Cathedral as a background, but it was dramatic just to have the rearing horse and Jackson's victory salute pictured against a cloudless sky.

When the phone rang I thought it was Ellen. "May I speak with Millie Chambers?" a soft female voice asked.

"This is she," I answered ... somebody selling something, no doubt.

"I'm Marléne Weathers. The cemetery custodian

gave me your card and note. My Aunt Helen is very anxious to learn what this is all about."

I almost dropped the phone. "We found something that belonged to someone named Marléne. There was a train ticket from nineteen thirty-three and a letter from Helen in Chicago to Marléne in New Orleans." I think I was babbling from excitement, but she had said "Aunt Helen" hadn't she? Could that be the Helen who had written the letter? Surely not after sixty years!

The voice interrupted. "Could we meet somewhere?"

"I don't have a car, can you come here?"

"Where's here?"

I gave her the address of my gallery, then I put everything away and pushed my cart at a run. "Miss Leona," I said in a rush, "I'm going to close the shop for a while. I'm having some important company and I need privacy!"

It was after four-thirty, according to my watch, so I decided to call Ellen. I wasn't supposed to call her house, and I never had, but this was important. She'd want to know.

My fingers were actually trembling as I dialed. The phone rang a couple of times then I heard, "Hello?" A woman's voice, weak and quavering... Ellen's mother, of course.

"Is Ellen there?" I asked.

"I'm afraid not. She and her husband aren't back from Dallas yet."

Chapter 13

How many times did she knock before I heard? When I finally opened the door she was turning away, ready to leave.

Her smile was cautious. "You're Millie Chambers?" she asked.

I nodded and held the door wide open so she could enter. I nodded again, trying to give her my attention, but the scream in my head was louder than the words her lips were forming. Married. My brain floundered. Ellen is married and in Dallas with her husband. She's in Dallas with her husband.

Sensing that something was not quite right, with some hesitation and a questioning frown, she held out my card and note. "What's this about?"

"Come," I said. I planned each step: walk to the kitchen table, bend, lift the suitcase away from the wall, place it on the table, open it, push it toward her. I couldn't make my eyes focus. Married . . . Ellen is married and in Dallas with her husband!

"Is this what you found? May I look through it?"

She waited for my nod. She pulled out a chair and sat with the suitcase in front of her. After a minute, she began removing the garments, one by one. There was nothing I could do except sit and watch. I didn't care anymore.

Before she opened the envelope she questioned me with her eyes. At my nod, which was all I could manage, she took out the letter and slowly read it. The contents didn't seem to faze her. She didn't look at the snapshot until the letter had been read. She held the photo up for better light and studied it for a long time.

Pointing to the dark-haired girl in the photo, she said in a whisper, "This is my Great-Aunt Helen. I've seen other pictures of her from that time." She looked over at me. "Tell me, please, how you came to have all this?"

Consciousness returned slowly. If I told her, maybe she'd leave. I cleared my throat and managed to get my lips moving. "We found the suitcase in Mississippi, in a hideaway along the coast where lots of liquor was stored." Trying to remember the how and why of the suitcase almost made me forget that my heart had stopped beating many minutes ago.

"The liquor and the suitcase have been hidden underground since prohibition ended."

The woman looked at the picture. "I was named for this Marléne." She pointed to the blond girl. "She and Great-Aunt Helen were lovers."

"I know," I said.

"How did you happen to find the hideaway?" Her eyes looked directly into mine. "And how did you find us?"

Who was "us"? She was here alone, and she was nowhere near as old as the Marléne in the picture would have to be. Letting that pass, I answered her question. "Hurricane Gertrude blew away part of the Mississippi coast, and I have a place over there. We just stumbled on it."

Without speaking she put everything back in the suitcase. "Would you let me take this to Aunt Helen? It would mean a great deal to her." Her expression was anxious; she was obviously dealing with a person who was not quite right, after all.

"Sure," I said, mute again and wondering why I could still breathe. It wasn't until I had closed the door behind her that I realized I had no name, no phone number, no address, and the suitcase had vanished as if we had never found it. While climbing my stairs I realized that I still didn't care.

The portrait of Ellen that I had done from memory was the first to go . . . then the nightgown and robe . . . then everything that belonged to her, everything that reminded me of her . . . everything

129

went into the trash. I went through each room throwing away memories, my tears unstoppable.

I am a fool, a gullible fool, I told myself. Now Ellen's comings and goings at odd hours began to make sense. Meetings, seminars, conferences. All lies. Everything about her was a lie, even when she said she loved me. That was the hardest cut of all because I believed her words of love. I fell on the bed, crying until I had no more tears to cry.

Discovering that even the walking dead have to eat, in the morning I went for chili at the hot dog place. It wasn't open. I tried the Café du Monde, which is always open, but it reminded me of Frank so I trudged back to the gallery.

Way past the time I should have been out on the square working, I was trying to choke down a sandwich and sharing a shady bench with an old, bearded, toothless man. He leered at me for a while before deciding to ask for money.

"Girlie, got any change?"

I turned my head and stared at him. I didn't speak, I just stared, unmoving. He probably thought I was putting the gris-gris on him. Shrinking away, he hobbled out to the street. When he turned to make sure I wasn't following, I could see his mouth moving. Whether praying or cursing, I didn't care.

From the corner of my eye I kept seeing Ellen walking the square but, of course, it wasn't she. Ellen was in Dallas with her husband. They were probably in a motel, and she was showing him the things we had done together.

My pain was gut deep and burning. I am not the most courageous person in the world, which explains why I didn't walk across the street and dive into the river. I will leave, I decided. Today I will pack my stuff and go. There's enough money in the bank for me to split, and that's what I'm going to do.

I walked back to my gallery, spoke with Miss Leona, told her I was closing and that if there was anything she wanted for her to feel free to take it. She didn't ask questions. Together we hung the Closed sign on my door. I called the Frame and Box Store in the next block and ordered boxes. I had been buying my frames from them for years so they knew me. No problem for them to deliver right away.

Most of the day I sorted and packed books. Each box was sealed and the contents listed. I planned to store everything but my money and my clothes. I had no close family, and even my distant relatives were very distant both in miles and blood ties. The frantic sorting and packing seemed to ease some of my pain. At nightfall I went back to the hot dog restaurant and had my first hot food of the day. On my way back to the gallery, I could hardly get my legs to move.

The phone hadn't been disconnected yet, so when it rang, I answered. Ellen wouldn't call me from Dallas so it had to be Lou.

"Bonnye and I are coming by for you, Millie. We want you to see our house." She hung up before I could tell her that I didn't want to see their house, that I was dirty and unbathed and too tired to think . . . and too heartsick.

Lou banged on the door with her fist. I opened it and waved them inside saying, "Everything's a mess because I've been packing all day."

"Packing," Lou echoed. "Why are you packing?"

"I'm leaving, Lou. Gonna get my ass out of here,

go someplace else." Tears were forming, and I fought to hold them back. "I'm through with New Orleans."

Lou's mouth opened in astonishment. Bonnye looked at me with wide eyes. Lou roared, "Millie, what in hell is going on? What's happened?" Now she was frowning, fists clenched, hands on her hips. "What is it, Millie?" she demanded.

I sat on a book-filled box and, unable to hold back, began bawling as if my heart was broken... which it was. What I was telling them must not have made sense because Lou sat beside me, put her arm across my shoulder, and bent to look in my face. "What are you saying about Ellen?" she asked.

Hearing Ellen's name made me bawl louder. Bonnye and Lou sat, one on each side, until my sobs were manageable. "Ellen is married," I said. "I called her house today, and her mother told me that Ellen and her husband were in Dallas. That's why I'm leaving."

"You didn't know she was married?" Bonnye asked in a tiny voice.

Lou's warning glance at Bonnye was a clue. "No," I answered, "did you?"

Lou took over. "I figured all along it was something like that, Millie, but you didn't seem to mind so I didn't say anything. Even Bonnye agreed with me, and she doesn't know Ellen all that good."

"You knew all this time?" My tears had stopped.

Lou shifted, her arm still around my shoulder, "Not really, but I couldn't figure any other explanation." She looked at me, her face as serious as I'd ever seen it. "You don't have to leave town, Millie. I don't think that'll make you happy at all.

You've got a good thing here; don't throw it away on account of Ellen."

"But she lied to me all along. I love her. I thought she loved me."

Bonnye nodded. "You'll get over it," she said earnestly. "Ellen's not the only fish in the sea." She seemed to be speaking from experience.

"If you're leaving so you won't have to see Ellen again, you're just being silly. Honestly, you have a great place to live and work, and this town is big enough that y'all won't run into each other." Lou got to her feet. "Please, Millie, don't go off half-cocked!"

Was that what I was doing? I only wanted to get away from the pain, and I was sure leaving would accomplish that in a hurry. I heaved myself off the box, looked up at Lou and down at Bonnye. "Thanks, but I've made up my mind."

Bonnye stood, and Lou gathered her in with both arms. Lou glared over Bonnye's head at me. "I'm not going to let you go," she said firmly. Releasing Bonnye, Lou lifted a box, peered at the label, and said, "These go upstairs, don't they?"

I shouted, "No, don't do that!" but Lou was already climbing. I heard Lou rip the cardboard lid, and books began thumping to the floor as she upended the box. I ran up the stairs to find her shoving books on one of the wall shelves.

"Come on, give me a hand," she said, looking over her shoulder at me. Paralyzed with indecision, I stood like a dummy while Lou stacked books by the handful, not looking to see if they were even partly arranged as books should be. Bonnye appeared with a small box that Lou tore open. When all the books were back on the shelves Lou and Bonnye went downstairs and tackled the paintings, hanging whatever was on top of the stack wherever there was a hanger. The gallery looked dreadful.

Kitchen things, like plates and glasses, were on the table waiting to go into a box. Lou swept everything up in an armful but then couldn't put anything down. She looked at me. "Get a move on," she growled, "I need help."

"Why am I doing this?" I asked of no one in particular as I placed things where I thought they belonged. My heart was still heavy and I did a lot of sniffing and sighing as work progressed, but not leaving New Orleans was infinitely less effort than leaving.

With the two of them moving at the speed of light, an hour at the most, my things were back in place — not the right place necessarily, but at least out of the boxes and off the floors. One plus to all this was that my books got dusted for the first time in four years.

"Do you have a cleaning lady?" Bonnye asked innocently.

I had to laugh, a reaction that would have been impossible only hours before. "Nope," I answered, "I can see that I need one."

Lou walked to the door and held it open. "Get moving," she said, gesturing with her hand, "I'm starving to death!"

"I can't go like this," Bonnye and I chorused at the same time, but we went anyway.

Over spaghetti, I told them about the woman and the suitcase, and we took turns guessing about "Aunt" Helen. We didn't mention Ellen even once. I actually drank two beers, resulting in a deathlike sleep as soon as my head touched the pillow.

Lou called before I was fully conscious. "Bonnye fixed breakfast for us. I'll pick you up in ten minutes."

Bonnye was a good cook, I found, but I also found that my heart hadn't healed overnight. My head was a lot clearer, but I had no answer when Lou asked me what I had intended to do with the camp when I left. I didn't know; I hadn't thought about it. "You could sell it to me," she said. "I could use it while I build on my property. Sell it later."

"I have to think about it," I said. "The camp has been my dream for so long, you know, that it's almost like a part of me." I pushed back my chair. "I'll probably have to get a car."

The next morning I called Miss Leona. She didn't ask one question about the horrendous mess in the gallery. We rehung the paintings in their proper places and, borrowing her vacuum, I did the gallery rug.

After lunch, when things were reasonably straight, I went out on the square. My first customer probably thought I had a terminal lung disease because I had to draw deep breaths so often.

As I sketched, I had imaginary conversations with Ellen. We would converse like ordinary humans at first; then I'd start screaming at her. She had betrayed me and I wanted to know why. What was her reason? Why couldn't she love me like I loved her? She must have known I'd find out some day. Then what? Those thoughts swirled around and around in my head, causing a depression so deep I packed my cart and left.

Lou and Bonnye were going to stick to me as long as they thought I needed their support, and I loved them for it. We ate that evening in a Greek restaurant. The wine caused my eyelids to shut without being told. The last thing I remember was leaning over the table to tell Bonnye that I thought I'd go to and from the camp by boat.

Bonnye was still working at the pipe place, but Lou could arrange to be in the quarter at noon, so I wasn't surprised when she showed up next to my cart. "Let's eat," she said. "I've got something to tell you."

We got a couple of po-boys from the grocery and settled on an unoccupied bench in the square. Eating was serious business, so we didn't talk until the last swallow. "I don't know exactly how to say this," Lou started, "but have you thought about AIDS?"

"Why should I think about that?"

Lou hung her head, clasped her hands, and stared at pigeons picking invisible things off the sidewalk. She spoke, but not in her usual rumble. "Ellen, I mean. Ellen and AIDS. It took a while for me to suspect she was married and, by then, I figured it was too late already."

"What are you talking about, Lou? Ellen doesn't have AIDS."

"Maybe not, Millie, but she's sleeping with a man, and you don't know that he isn't sleeping around, do you?"

No, I didn't know. I didn't even know his name. I had never once thought about the three of us sharing body fluids, but that's what I'd been doing, having sex with a woman who had sex with a man who could have screwed half of Louisiana.

Picturing Frank, I swallowed hard. "Lou, I don't want to think about anything like that. I simply can't handle it right now."

When the phone rang Friday night I was afraid it was Ellen. "Yes," I answered, my heart racing. It was Ellen.

"Millie, I have to see you. I'm coming over."

"Don't bother," I said and hung up. The phone rang again and again but I didn't answer. There was nothing I wanted to say.

Chapter 14

There was no possible way to avoid Ellen. If she wanted to see me, I was exposed to the world when I worked the square. At night I was available in the gallery except when I locked up and went to bed. And I had to answer my phone because someone could be calling about a painting.

It was no surprise when I saw her walking across Chartres Street the next morning, heading straight for me. I wasn't busy at that moment, so I just sat and watched every step as she approached. Close up she looked haggard, and her eyes were red. I pulled away when she put her hand on my arm.

"Get away from me," I hissed.

"Millie, please, you don't understand." She touched me again.

"I understand that I don't want anything to do with you, so leave me alone!" I don't know where I got the strength, but I slid my feet to the ground, pushed from the chair, and walked away.

She was behind me. "Please," she said again. "Millie, let me explain!" She held my shoulder.

Turning, I looked directly into her eyes and snarled, "Get your cheating hands off." I jerked away and started walking, blinded by the tears that filled my eyes.

"Millie," she called. I didn't turn.

Trembling all over, I slammed into the gallery, almost knocking Miss Leona to the floor. I half expected Ellen to be behind me, but she wasn't. After an hour, when I was calmer, I went back to the square.

Lou appeared that afternoon as I was closing my cart. She helped with my umbrella and the chairs, kindly pretended not to notice my eyes that, by that time, had to be as red as Rudolph's nose. We stored the cart in the kitchen. I settled with Miss Leona, who was giving me funny looks, and followed Lou to her truck.

"Ellen came by, didn't she?" I huddled next to the window, my feet resting on empty paint cans. I nodded.

"Thought so." Lou slammed the shift, causing us to lurch forward. "You knew she would, didn't you?"

I nodded again.

"What did you say?"

It was a minute before I could answer. "I told her to get away from me and she did."

"Then why are you crying, Millie? Wasn't that what you wanted?"

"I guess." I had been ready to run out of town to get away from Ellen, so weren't my tears unnecessary? "I guess," I said again. I had gotten what I wanted, hadn't I?

A few days later as I slammed my gallery door behind me the, phone started ringing. Let it be Ellen, I thought as I raced to pick it up. Don't let it be Ellen, I thought as I held the receiver to my ear.

It was Marléne. "Would you have time to meet Aunt Helen tomorrow? She lives on Esplanade near City Park, and she's very anxious to talk with you. Would after supper be okay, say seven o'clock?"

"I don't have a car. Could you come for me?" I didn't think that was unreasonable.

"Sure," she said easily. "Is it okay if I toot? I don't think I could find a parking place."

She was driving a low-slung red car that looked like it cost more than I made in ten years. I had to fold myself into the front seat. "Belt," she said briefly, giving me a sideways glance. While I fumbled with a tangle of webbing she looked at me again. "Did you do all the paintings I saw in your gallery?"

"Yes," I answered, wishing she'd keep her eyes on the road and not on me.

"They're great!" she said. "You're pretty talented, you know."

"Thank you." I have been told that many times. It's what puts food on my table.

There was no more talking until we stopped in front of a huge three-story home with white columns. She either lives in a nursing home or Aunt Helen is rich, I said to myself as we walked up the steps. Marléne used a key to open one of the ornate glass doors, and we walked down a quiet hall to a door at the end.

An elderly woman was sitting in a rocker, a lap robe over her knees, and as Marléne introduced us, she held out her hand. In my oversized paw her blue-veined hand was lost, but I felt her squeeze.

Looking up, she smiled at me and I saw, or imagined I saw, a flash of resemblance to the dark-haired girl in the photo. "How kind of you to come," she said, withdrawing her hand.

Motioning me to the chair in front of her she said, "Now, tell me how you came by this suitcase?"

I glanced at Marléne, who sat on a low stool next to Aunt Helen's chair. She was smiling as if, in me, she had caught the gold ring. I cleared my throat and told them the story. They were both very intent on my words, and Aunt Helen sat back with a sigh when I finished.

Clutching Marléne's hand, she said in a voice full of wonder, "She was coming to meet me, I know that now." I saw tears begin to gather. "I would have kept her safe."

Marléne's tears were streaming. "Please don't cry," she begged. "Now you know for sure that she loved you. Isn't that so?" she asked, looking at me. "The train ticket proves it!"

Tears were becoming easy. I wiped at mine and said, "They must have killed her just before she left for Chicago."

I was partly in shock because the woman who had written the letter sixty years ago was sitting in front of me and I had never imagined such a thing. The letter writer had been a young woman deeply in love and waiting to rejoin the lover who never came.

"You've read my letter; now read hers." Aunt Helen handed me three thin envelopes, faded and much handled. I read every word then handed them back. "She really loved you, Aunt Helen." I took that liberty out of respect because I couldn't call her just Helen.

"Yes," Aunt Helen nodded, "I believe the pain is going now that I know. We dreamed of having a life together, and I thought she had forsaken me."

"I don't know why you went to so much trouble to find the suitcase owner, but we'll be eternally grateful." Marléne looked up at Aunt Helen, who was nodding. "Do you think we could keep it?" She was pointing to the suitcase next to Aunt Helen's chair.

"It doesn't belong to me," I explained. "My friend found it on her property, but I'll bet she'll be happy to let Aunt Helen have it. After all, if things had worked out as planned, the suitcase would have gone to Chicago with Marléne, wouldn't it?"

It seemed the most natural thing in the world for me to be talking about lesbian love with two women whom I didn't know. At no time had I ever been that open. Both Marléne and Aunt Helen seemed to take it for granted that I understood and approved. For that matter, I did understand the pain of losing someone you loved. I had lost Ellen, but who's to say she was ever really mine?

"May I give you something, dear?" Aunt Helen seemed tired. I didn't want anything from her but couldn't disappoint her by saying no, so I nodded. As if they had discussed it, Marléne opened the suitcase and handed Aunt Helen one of the handkerchiefs, which Aunt Helen put in my hand. "I embroidered this for Marléne. I'd like for you to have it."

Too choked to say a word, I nodded again. As I took the delicate white cloth from her hand I smelled again the faint, sweet odor that was Marléne's.

"Would you like to have a drink somewhere?" The car was moving at a normal speed. Marléne kept looking at me, but I was overcome with emotion and hadn't spoken since we'd left Aunt Helen asleep in her chair, a tiny white handkerchief in her hand.

"I guess so," I finally managed. "I don't drink, so could we have coffee or tea instead?" Foolish. Coffee and tea are drinks.

Somewhere near the lake Marléne pulled through ornate gates into a parking area. She got out of the car and motioned for me to follow. I thought we were going into a residence but, once past an empty hallway, we entered a spacious room full of small tables and so dimly lit I was stumbling into things. Like a mole, Marléne led me confidently through darkness to a table for two. It was near a wall, I think, and the candle flame flickering through lavender glass sucked in more light than it gave out.

"Where are we?" I asked in a hushed voice, leaning so that she could hear me.

"It's strictly for women," she said. "I thought you'd like it here."

I was leading with my chin but I asked, "Why did

you think I'd enjoy this place?" My tone wasn't belligerent, just curious.

"You're a lesbian, aren't you?"

Our waitress must have used radar to find us. I ordered tea, Marléne ordered tea. I think, if not for me, she would have had something much stronger. While I sugared my tea I answered her question. "Yes, I am."

"Are you with anyone?"

"No, not at present." The tea was strong enough to fuel a rocket.

"I'm single too. Hell, isn't it?"

The answer to that was obvious, so I changed the subject. "Where are we? There were no signs or other clues."

"This is a very private club . . . good food, good drinks, a dance floor, and rooms upstairs. We only bring very special guests." I think she pointed at me. "You're extra special because of what you've done for Aunt Helen. I'm indebted to you."

I started to say, "Aw shucks," but Marléne was serious so I said instead, "It's hard for me to believe Aunt Helen's been in love with a dead woman for sixty years."

"She's been in love with a memory, not a dead woman. Aunt Helen left home to be with Marléne. They had loved each other for years, and going to Chicago was the only way they could share their lives. Think about it. Sixty years ago women married because it was all there was. Aunt Helen went to Chicago first because she was the most daring. Marléne was to meet her, only Marléne never came."

"She's been putting flowers on Marléne's grave for sixty years?"

"Not hard to believe. When Aunt Helen gave up and came home, her father bought her a small flower shop near the cemeteries. Even though he was my relative, he was a horrible man. He disowned Aunt Helen, but she made a success of the shop. I own it now. We send flowers monthly, but I take red roses on special occasions. But you knew that, didn't you? That's how you found us."

"I'm glad I didn't give up."

"So is Aunt Helen. We've talked for days, and she has touched everything in the suitcase at least a dozen times. The only thing we didn't talk about was the way Marléne died."

"Who did it? Do you know? And why?"

"No. It might have had something to do with Marléne's uncle, but no one knows. Would you like more tea?"

The waitress was standing at my side. I peered, saying, "No, thank you." While we were talking the room had almost filled with women. Soft music, the hum of conversation, and the sound of low laughter was intoxicating. I had never been in a place like that.

Marléne was smiling at me. "Would you like to dance?" she asked softly.

In the darkness she couldn't possibly see me blush. I hesitated, wanting to but not wanting to. She stood and took my hand. "This way," she said, winding her way across the room.

Who leads, I wondered. She did. She held me close against her; I could feel her warmth. Ellen and I had never danced, I thought; we only made love. As Marléne shifted against me, I imagined Ellen's body close and inviting. How nice it would be to hold her again, husband or no. I let the music carry me away. The music, a woman's arms, her leg pressing between mine caused arousal so acute I stopped moving.

Marléne's lips were soft, her mouth sweet. We held each other, unmindful of the women moving in a slow rhythm around us. "We can go upstairs," Marléne whispered.

The stairs were carpeted, the hall was carpeted, and the door opened without a sound. We stepped into what would have been an ordinary bedroom except for a mirrored ceiling. Marléne led me into the bathroom and flicked on the lights. I gawked at my image reflected in the mirrored walls that surrounded the Jacuzzi on three sides.

She leaned to open the upper drawer of a dressing table. "See," she said.

I recognized dental dams ... it was written on the box ... but had no idea what the other boxes and bottles contained.

"It's not a house rule or anything, but it's smart to practice safe sex these days, don't you think?"

I nodded because it was smart and because she had everything we probably needed as protection right there in that drawer. I had been ready to leap on her when we entered the room, but now I felt desire beginning to fade.

Marléne sensed this. "Come," she said softly. Back in the bedroom, not speaking, she undressed me, then herself. Desire returned with a flash when she pressed against me. Her warm hands and soft mouth on my breasts made my heart race. I was ready again.

* * * * *

"Who's Ellen?" Marléne murmured. I could only blink. She rolled over to cover my body with hers and gave a short laugh. "I hope you didn't have to get home early; it's past three now."

"Don't care." I wrapped my legs around hers. She lifted on both elbows, leaned to lick my breasts again with her talented tongue. "I'm thirsty," she said. "I'm going to order something to drink."

I watched her walk to the phone. She spoke to someone then returned to the bed, evading my outstretched arms. "You can have me again in about five minutes," she said. It couldn't have been that long before I heard a soft knock. Completely naked, Marléne opened the door and picked up a tray.

"This is some kind of place," I said after gulping ice cold tea.

"We like it," Marléne said, taking my hand. "Fucking in the shower is fun. Shall we?"

Decatur Street was filling with tourists. I leaned down into the car window and said, "I enjoyed last night."

Marléne touched my cheek. "Let's do it again?"

"Sure, you have my number."

I watched the car roar to a squealing stop at the corner of Decatur then, narrowly missing two pedestrians, cut into the moving traffic.

Chapter 15

I had certainly enjoyed sex with Marléne even if it meant that I had to prop my eyes open with toothpicks the entire next day. My yawns were becoming so frequent that I closed early and went upstairs for a nap. I hoped my snores wouldn't disturb Miss Leona or customers, if she had any.

She had closed the gallery, leaving me asleep, so I slept blissfully on until Lou's fist banging on my door awakened me. "We weren't sure you were home," she thundered when I let them in.

"I'm here," I said. "I'm here and hungry. A quick shower and I'll be ready."

Lou drove us to West End for seafood. After eating until we could eat and talk at the same time, she asked about Helen and Marléne. They were awed, too, when I described Aunt Helen and her sixty-year vigil. Lou felt proud that she'd found the underground cache and agreed instantly that Aunt Helen could keep the suitcase. "After all," she pointed out, "if Marléne had gone to Chicago instead of getting killed, the suitcase would have gone north with her, right?" She waited for confirmation.

Bonnye and I nodded solemnly, agreeing that's what would have happened. "What's this Marléne like?" Bonnye asked.

"Well," I thought about Marléne before I answered, "I think she's probably a few years older than I, very attractive, and much richer than I'll ever be. She's also very nice."

"Do you think we ought to tell about the money in the suitcase? I could give it back, you know." Lou is an honest person.

"No. I told them, and Aunt Helen said she didn't want any money."

"Y'all were out pretty late last night; I know because I kept calling." Lou is curious, too.

"Marléne picked me up at my place around seven and drove me to Aunt Helen's house. From there we went to a private lesbian club. We danced a while and then we went to bed." It wasn't easy to keep a serious expression, but I managed.

Bonnye recovered first. With complete composure she said, "I guess that means you're getting over Ellen?"

149

Lou, who has known me longer, was still in shock.

"Bonnye, I hope so. Marléne and I did seem to hit it off." Now I had to grin, and Bonnye grinned back.

Her brown eyes sparkling, Bonnye said, "If you're not seeing her tomorrow, will you eat with us?"

"Sure," I answered. I loved them both for trying to keep me too busy for loneliness. It behooved me to stay home and finish a commission, but what the heck, I thought. I'm free and almost thirty; I deserve to be good to myself.

On the way out to the car Bonnye asked if Ellen had called or come by. The sharp pain I felt had nothing to do with gastrointestinal upset. I don't think Bonnye was being nosy; she was genuinely concerned.

"I haven't heard from her since she came by the square that day, and I hope I don't hear from her again." I was as serious as I knew how to be.

Bonnye didn't comment until we were in the car heading back to the quarter. She was snuggled against Lou, but I heard her clearly. "I think you'd feel better if you talked with her."

"If she phones, I'll talk. But I'm not going to call her." I'd die before I'd call, but I'm dying anyway, I thought.

For the next few days I went late to the square and quit early, my energy level so low I could hardly push my cart. When Marléne stopped by I was busy trying to restock, but I agreed to have a drink with her.

"Aunt Helen has asked about you, Millie. I told her we didn't see each other often, and she made me promise to do something about that. I wanted to call but we've had a half dozen evening weddings that I had to decorate personally." She drove through gates I recognized and put her hand on my thigh when the car stopped. "I intend to do something about that now," she promised.

Yes, we had a drink. Yes, we danced. We also climbed the stairs.

A day or two later Marléne called to tell me she enjoyed fishing from the seawall. "The lake's calm, the breeze is constant, and the fish occasionally bite. Let's go, shall we?"

We picked our spot under a straggly tree, spread a blanket, and lay back to watch the clouds. "When do we fish?" I asked.

"When I was little my parents brought me here often. They'd say 'Let's go fishing,' and here's where we'd end up, on a blanket just like this." She sat up and looked down at me. "So, my dear Millie, what we're doing is fishing."

She was smiling, and I liked what I saw. We were in public but, except for cars passing on Lakeshore Drive, there was no one in sight for two blocks. She leaned for a quick kiss, and I liked that, too.

We lay without talking, watching the sky dim. I must have sighed because she said quietly, "Ellen, again?"

"Of course not. Why did you say that? For that matter, what do you know about Ellen?" I was close to being angry.

"I don't know anything. It's just that I've heard her name and at the most inopportune time."

"What's that supposed to mean?"

"When we fuck, you thrash about like a bear in a trap and sometimes you say 'Ellen.' That's all. I can't help wondering."

I sighed again because it seemed Ellen and I were a closed book that wouldn't stay shut. "She's someone I used to love," I said. "I think about her once in a while, that's all."

"No, Millie dear, you think about her a lot. I know how it is because I just ended an eight-year love affair with a woman I think about even when I'm making love with you. My heart is actually broken into a million pieces, and I don't think it'll ever get back together." Marléne sat up, smiled ruefully, and said, "Aunt Helen knows about the breakup, but she doesn't know why it had to be. She keeps telling me that love is precious and shouldn't be thrown away."

"Aunt Helen knows you're gay?"

"Of course. We lived in her third-floor apartment for most of our eight years. She knows everything there is to know except why. And it's the why that's killing me."

If Marléne thought about her ex-partner when we made love, then it was only fair to admit that I thought about Ellen. "Marléne, I think I fell into bed with you because I wanted Ellen and she's not available. See, she forgot to tell me she's married and living with her husband."

We were sitting facing each other, and I could tell Marléne was in pain. She touched at the tears on her cheeks. "How awful," she sniffed. "Is there hope?"

"No. It's over, but I still love her." At last I had

said it. "It's over, but I still love her." Bonnye had known it before I did.

"I still love Eva, too. I had no idea there was anything going on, but when the silver disappeared as well as the money in our bank account, I got suspicious."

"Why did she need money?" From what I could see, Marléne had more than enough for two.

"She had a girlfriend. I had forgotten something one morning so I drove home and caught them making love in our bed. It was probably still warm from my being in it." Marléne put her head in her hands. "The woman had gone down on her and Eva was saying things and making sounds I'd never heard. I actually stood in the doorway and heaved."

"Did you know the woman?"

"That's what I don't understand. She was young, trashy, and didn't have a pot or a window. Yet Eva was supporting her and had been for months. I think the woman was on drugs because you could have bought a house with what Eva took. I kicked them both out."

"Marléne, eight years is a lot of time to throw away. Have you been in touch with her?" Didn't Bonnye ask me if I'd been in touch with Ellen? Maybe it's just a generic question everybody asks.

"She talked with Aunt Helen when I wouldn't answer her calls, but I don't know what she said. There's no telling." Marléne was shaking her head. "I changed the locks and the phone listing, got her name off of all our legal papers, and gave her stuff to Goodwill. That erased her so far as I'm concerned."

"Then you're on the prowl, aren't you?"

"Not any more." She looked at me knowingly.

"I'm not over Ellen," I said quickly. "I think it'll take more time." For all her sophistication, Marléne was hurting the same way I was. She was fun to be with, and great in bed, but I didn't think she was ready for another love affair either, with me or anyone else.

"I can wait," she said.

It was dark. The lights had come on, and the wind was brisk and cold. We folded our blanket and walked to the car. "I need a bathroom," Marléne explained, as we turned in to huge gates that I recognized.

"Shall I wait here for you?" I asked, even as I opened my door.

"Of course not," Marléne spoke laughingly. She held the back door for me and we walked directly upstairs.

"You may call me Ellen if it helps," she breathed, sliding her hand beneath my shirt. "I want to show you what that woman was doing to Eva. Do you mind?"

No, I didn't mind at all. Soon, Marléne's warm mouth and the pressure of her breasts against mine made me want sex so much I began tearing at my clothes. She touched between my legs, and I felt moisture oozing. Her hands were warm on my naked flesh. Her soft tongue circling my clitoris and spreading the sticky wetness drove me out of my mind.

We stopped downstairs to have a drink on the way out. The room was as dark as ever, and there was a scattering of women, some on the dance floor, some at tables. I ordered my usual tea, but this time I asked the waitress if I could have it somewhat weaker. "And a glass of water, please." I'd doctor it myself if necessary.

"We seem to do fine in bed, don't we?" Marléne was having a cocktail this time, something with an olive. Either that or an eyeball, I couldn't tell. "You actually remembered that my name was Marléne," she teased.

Our waitress put two glasses in front of me but I couldn't tell which glass held tea and which held water. Just to be sure, I sugared both. "I was trying really hard," I confessed. "Because, by the time we hit the bed, I was already flying as you no doubt could tell. Honestly, Marléne, there's something about fishing that sets me off!"

She reached across the table and found my hand. "I like you, Millie. I like you a lot."

"The feeling's mutual, but I don't think it'll go beyond that." No use buying into something that I didn't think I'd want after I got it. "There's nothing wrong with you, it's me. I'm still in love with Ellen and I can't see that changing any time soon." And then, too, I thought, I really wouldn't want to hurt you; you've been hurt enough.

She sipped her drink, then said, "What about the sex, Millie? You enjoy it as much as I do." She was still touching my hand.

"Maybe even more," I confessed. No use lying. We were just fine in bed together, but we were both good mechanics. Marléne and I had been servicing each other's sexual needs, we weren't in love.

"I hope this doesn't mean we won't see each other again. Aunt Helen wants you to have dinner with us very soon, and I would like to bed you again." She lifted my hand. "These are such wonderful fingers for fucking."

Remembering where those wonderful fingers had been not half an hour before, I blushed into the darkness.

I often did oil portraits from photographs and had agreed to put an entire family of five together on one canvas using separate photos of each family member. That would take many days to complete, but it would pay my rent for a couple of months.

Lou and Bonnye came over to sit nights while I worked. There was still some decorating to do in their new house, but they were waiting it out with me. We had not been to the camp for many weeks. The place would only remind me of Ellen, anyway.

"You know I didn't get that place in Mississippi, Millie," Lou announced. "There was a lot of confusion about ownership, so it went off the block until that could be cleared up. If you're not going to be using your place, then I don't want that land, anyway."

"But, Lou, you and Bonnye would have enjoyed building a place over there. Tell you what" — I made an instant decision — "I'll sell you half the camp and we can share. You and Bonnye can have the big bedroom and I'll take the small one. Bonnye, you're good at decorating, how does that sound?"

Bonnye hugged me and kissed my cheek. "I love it," she said. "Lou, can we do it?"

"Whatever you want, honey. I like the idea, too."

Lou would have bought the sun, the moon, and

the stars if Bonnye decided she had a use for them. "Then I guess it's settled," I said.

Over the weeks Lou had slimmed down. I attributed it to the frequency of their lovemaking, remembering Ellen and me in the beginning, but Bonnye was doing the cooking and she had Lou dieting. Lou was eating right for the first time in her life . . . eating right and enjoying it. They were so right for each other that it almost hurt to watch them.

"Would you want to go to the camp this weekend, Millie? The woodwork still needs another coat, you remember, and Bonnye swings a mean brush."

"Okay, Lou, I'm game if you are." It would be hell without Ellen, I knew. Maybe I'd ask Marléne. She might enjoy it. "Would you guys mind if I invited Marléne?"

They looked at each other and then back at me. "No," they chorused. "That's great!"

I stared up at my skylight, wide awake and hurting from wanting to hold Ellen. This can't go on forever, I thought. Everybody says it takes time to get over a love affair, but they don't say how much time.

How nice it would be if I could fall in love with Marléne. She was falling in love with me, I knew. We still visited the upstairs rooms, and I enjoyed the sex. But it was a release of sexual tension, not an act of love. Marléne understood this, too.

Chapter 16

Marléne said she would be delighted to go with us to Mississippi Saturday morning. "I'll have to leave around three Sunday because I have a late afternoon wedding. Will that cause a problem?"

"Not at all. We'll go in two cars." And that's what we did. Marléne, following my directions, pulled into the driveway way ahead of Lou and Bonnye. We had all the windows open and were making the bed in the small bedroom when we heard Lou's Lincoln crunching gravel.

I had assumed that Lou and Bonnye wouldn't

need to go to a motel, so I wasn't surprised when Lou dumped their things in the bedroom Ellen and I had shared. Marléne and Bonnye made that bed while Lou and I carried the food upstairs.

The hallway gave me pause because it was the last thing Ellen had painted, and I could hear echoes of the laughter we had shared that day. Maybe I should sell the whole place to Lou because of all the memories I'd rather forget.

The four of us walked the beach, up to our ankles in water with sand squishing between our toes. Marléne thought the beach was a wonderful place to relax until we described the houses and the roads that had been blown away. "You believe in living dangerously, don't you?" she asked me.

"I figure it'll be at least fifty years before another blow like Gertrude. I'll take my chance." I knew she wasn't referring to the hurricane. I winked to show I understood.

Lou had brought steaks again. One would have been more than enough for the four of us, but she fired up the barbecue and covered the grill end-to-end and side-to-side with steak. She did a credible job with the cooking, and we gorged until steak was coming out of our ears. It was a fun time, and Marléne fit in like an old friend.

Bedtime came, and we said our goodnights. I had not slept with Marléne, we had only had sex, so I didn't know what to expect. When her hands began to roam my body I whispered that the walls were thin and that we'd best just go to sleep.

"Umm, I don't think so," she whispered back. "I came prepared." Her hand slipped inside my pajama bottoms, and her fingers began spreading the moisture she found between my legs. Of course, the more her fingers moved the wetter I became. To give her room, never mind the thinness of the walls, I shimmied out of my pajamas and spread my legs their widest.

"Should I stop?" she asked. I answered by pulling her face to mine. Understanding my need, she began thrusting her tongue in my mouth to match the thrusting motion of her fingers. My body went up like a rocket. Engulfed by wave after wave of pleasure, I could no more have stopped my loud cry than I could have stopped the sun.

"I thought we had to be quiet," Marléne said in a normal tone. "You said the walls were thin."

"They are," I answered. "Now pull those down, please." I helped her remove both top and bottom. I went down on her. She was ready, so very ready.

"Did you sleep well?" Bonnye asked at breakfast, barely concealing her smile with a piece of toast. Lou kept her head down, her plate of eggs and grits totally engrossing.

"I guess you heard that we did," I answered. They would have to be deaf not to have heard our bedsprings dancing most of the night. Bonnye seemed pleased. Having sex with Marléne meant I was getting over Ellen.

"Even if you aren't buying the place, would you like to show Marléne where we found the suitcase?" I had just washed dishes and was drying my hands. I turned to the table for their answer when Marléne's mobile phone rang. Marléne talked for a moment and the color drained from her face. She snapped the phone shut and pushed her chair from the table.

"Aunt Helen had a stroke, I have to go!"

"Want me to go with you?" I asked.

"No, she's not expected to live more than another hour or so and there'll be things for me to do. I'll see you back home."

She grabbed her purse from the bedroom and took off, the little car a flash of color on the road.

For the rest of the day Lou and I attempted to clear some of the builder's trash beneath the camp. We made piles of burnables, lit huge fires, and watched them burn down to ashes. Lou was very quiet, animated only when Bonnye was near. Once, when Lou was upstairs, I asked Bonnye what was the matter.

"I think Lou is embarrassed when you speak openly about, ah, about sex. I don't think the two of you talked very much to each other about being lesbians." She shrugged, "We heard you last night, you know, and Lou has to work through these things in her own way. She loves you, Millie. Just give her time."

Bonnye was young, and I wondered how she could see to the heart of a problem so fast. "About last night," I said, to begin an explanation.

Bonnye put her finger to her lips, "Shhh, you don't have to say anything. Honest."

"But, Bonnye, it's not how it looks. Marléne and I are having sex with each other because we can, that's all. She's going through heartbreak because her longtime lover was unfaithful and, well, you know about me. I still love Ellen." I found my throat getting tight. "I still love her with all my heart."

161

Somehow it was easy to explain to Bonnye what I couldn't say to Lou.

Bonnye looked at me and slowly shook her head. "I don't understand you, Millie."

"What's to understand?" I asked.

"If you love Ellen, why don't you talk with her? Maybe you'd feel different if you heard what she had to say."

"Bonnye, I know I'm scrawny and ugly and don't have a lot going for me, but I'm honest. I try to deal honestly with everybody, and I wouldn't cheat if you paid me. Ellen wasn't honest with me. She cheated and lied every minute we were together, and I just couldn't take it anymore, once I knew." Those damn tears were starting again. I wiped my face on my sleeve. "I hurt so much I think I'd be better off dead!"

"Oh, shit," Bonnye said. She moved in front of me and put her hands on my arms. "You're not thinking of doing anything foolish, are you?"

"Naw, I didn't really mean that. There's no way I'd hurt myself on purpose. It's just that I feel so terrible all the time."

"Last night you didn't feel terrible," she reminded me.

I had to smile. Yes, last night we had fucked our heads off and it had felt pretty good. But where was that glow I should be feeling today? "You're right. Last night I didn't feel terrible at all."

"It's late, and we should start getting ready to go. Lou hates to drive in that heavy coast traffic, you know."

I was home early enough to paint, so I locked myself in and started sketching a few swamp scenes. Tourists buy paintings of slow-moving bayous with moss-hung oaks and tiny wooden shacks up on stilts. I usually add a lighted lantern in the cabin's single window. The bayou's dark water reflects the lantern's light, adding a splash of yellow to the dark greens and browns.

Monday was very slow both on the square and in the gallery, so I took down my things when the crowd thinned to a few tired tourists. Marléne hadn't answered my call. The people at her flower shop said she was still at the hospital, that Aunt Helen was hanging on but still wasn't expected to live. Not wanting to intrude, I didn't call the hospital.

Miss Leona was glad to go home early. It had been a boring day for her, too. On the off chance that I might make a sale I left the Open sign in the window. I was eating chili at my kitchen table when I heard the tinkle that meant someone had come in. I wiped the chili from my mouth and walked to the front wearing the pasted-on smile appropriate for the occasion.

Ellen was quietly closing the door as I stepped into the gallery. I heard the lock snap as she turned the bolt and faced me. We stared, and my heart began thumping like a drum. I wanted to say the things I had rehearsed, but my mouth refused to open. She took a step forward and, when I didn't back away, took another step. Then she stopped.

"Millie," she said almost in a whisper.

I held out my hand. "Ellen," I said. She took

another step, and her hand reached mine. We stood, hands touching, neither moving until she asked, "Will you listen to me now?"

Nodding, I motioned to the love seat. She sat facing me, her hands unsteady in her lap. I didn't think her explanation would change anything, but her nearness made my heart ache.

"It wasn't a trip to Dallas with my husband. I was in Mexico establishing residence." She spoke as if the conversation I'd had with her mother had happened yesterday. "My divorce became final, and I flew home only to hear that you had called my house. I came here to explain, but you wouldn't listen." She was wringing her hands. "Your love had turned to hate, and I couldn't bear that I had caused you that much pain so I walked out of your life, my darling. You deserved so much better."

"I felt betrayed, Ellen. You lied to me from the start."

She looked down at her lap. "I know," she said. "It wasn't meant to be like that. I was attracted to you from the first, and I could see that you wanted me. That you were sexually aroused, just too shy to act." We stared at each other, the specter of shared sex as palpable as if we were naked and fucking that very moment.

Swallowing hard I asked, "Why did you deceive me, Ellen?"

"It wasn't planned. I had tried to make my marriage work, but he sensed my growing dissatisfaction in bed. We stopped having sex and he began getting it anyplace and anytime." She paused, swallowing hard. "Almost three years ago he tested HIV positive, and he decided I was at fault for denying him. My guilt was so complete I felt I had to stay. I didn't think there was any need to explain all this to you. Then we became lovers, and being with you was the only real thing in my life."

"Was that when you drew away from me? When you started breaking my heart piece by piece?" I may not have understood but I had to know.

"Yes, I hated the deception but I could find no way out for me, and I couldn't bear hurting you. I had fallen in love with you, Millie, so deeply in love that I was only alive when you held me."

"Why didn't you tell me then?"

"Would you have listened?" Her tight smile said that I would not have listened. "You're so straight," we both smiled at that, "so straight that your reaction would have been just what it was." She leaned and put her hand on my knee. I covered her hand with mine.

"Those few weeks we were apart were so painful I finally found the courage to act. Life without you would have been no life at all, so I told him I was going to get a divorce. He objected at first then asked me to wait for a few weeks so he could take care of some legal matters." She took my hand in both of hers, holding tight.

"Of course, I agreed," she continued. "I began to believe that soon I would be free and that you and I might have a life together so I drove across town in my nightgown. Remember?"

Yes, I remembered that night and the happiness I

felt when her arms enclosed me. I remembered that my broken heart had healed instantly and completely with her first kiss. I lifted her hand to my lips.

She pulled her hand away. "Please, Millie," she said. "You need to know it all."

I took her hand again because her words were stirring in me a feeling of such joy that breathing became difficult. As she began to speak I saw her eyes brim with tears.

"Before I met you I had already tested HIV negative for the second time, so I went to a lawyer for legal counsel. The quickest way was Mexico, I learned, so that's where I went. I didn't tell Mother, of course, nor you. I lied to her because she's old and ill, and I said nothing to you because I would only be gone three days at the most. I was going to surprise you." Her short laugh was without humor. "I almost got fired because I had been taking off so much time to be with you. But I'm free now, Millie."

The phone had been ringing for minutes. I've never considered myself to be psychic, and my premonitions are seldom confirmed, but I knew without a doubt that Marléne was calling to tell me Aunt Helen had died.

I released Ellen's hand, saying, "I have to answer that. It's Marléne calling to tell me Aunt Helen has passed away."

Ellen blinked in astonishment. She didn't know about Marléne or that we had located the original Helen. My call to give her this information was what caused our breakup in the first place.

"I'll fill you in later," I said. Then I walked to the kitchen phone. It was Marléne.

"Aunt Helen's dead, Millie. She died a few

minutes ago, and we heard her whisper the name Marléne. I was the only one in the room who knew that she was young again and that her beloved Marléne had finally come to begin their life together. Everyone else thought she meant me." Marléne was sobbing.

"I'm so sorry. Is there anything Ellen and I can do?" Might as well let her know Ellen and I are together again.

"No, dear, I'll call tomorrow. Aunt Helen felt close because you gave her back her dream. I'll always be grateful to you for doing that." I could still hear her sobbing as she hung up.

Ellen was as still as a statue on the love seat, her back straight, her hands clasped. I sat beside her, conscious of the warmth of her thigh against mine. "I have never stopped loving you, Ellen. Even when I sent you away, I loved you."

"I know the way I handled everything was stupid. Can you forgive me?" She had tears flowing, Marléne had been bawling, my own tears were streaming. I didn't find that tears changed anything, but they did help.

Right there on a love seat in front of a plate glass display window I kissed her. When our tongues met, I felt an electric shock that almost raised me off the seat. I tasted her mouth, felt her hands cup my face, and the kiss deepened. We didn't draw apart for many minutes.

"Yes, Millie, I want you, too," she said. No words were spoken as we climbed my spiral stair. Still not speaking we embraced. Standing by my bed, the skylight above us bright with light, we clung, not moving, just holding.

We made love, too. We were gentle with each other. Every inch of my body responded to Ellen's delicate touch. Later I stroked her slowly, tenderly touching every part of her. "I love you, Ellen," I whispered.

"Yes, my baby, yes," she answered.

We woke to a bright world of sunshine overhead. My sleep had been calm, restful, and Ellen was beside me, her warm body snuggled against mine.

"Coffee?" she said.

"I don't think I have any."

"Want to go out?" Her breath tickled my ear.

"No, I want to stay here." I stretched, yawning widely. I asked, "Do you have to go to school? It's probably too late already."

"Let's sleep in, okay?"

"I have to make two quick phone calls." I walked naked down to the kitchen phone.

"Miss Leona, don't come in today. I'll call you later."

Then I dialed Lou's house. Bonnye answered and I said, "Bonnye, did you call Ellen?"

"Yes," she answered. "You weren't going to do it, so somebody had to."

"Thank you," I said. Then I went back upstairs.

A few of the publications of
THE NAIAD PRESS, INC.
P.O. Box 10543 • Tallahassee, Florida 32302
Phone (904) 539-5965
Toll-Free Order Number: 1-800-533-1973
Mail orders welcome. Please include 15% postage.
Write or call for our free catalog which also features an
incredible selection of lesbian videos.

SMOKE AND MIRRORS by Pat Welch. 224 pp. 5th Helen Black
Mystery.   ISBN 1-56280-143-0 $10.95

DANCING IN THE DARK edited by Barbara Grier & Christine
Cassidy. 272 pp. Erotic love stories by Naiad Press authors.
                                                ISBN 1-56280-144-9   14.95

TIME AND TIME AGAIN by Catherine Ennis. 176 pp. Passionate
love affair.   ISBN 1-56280-145-7   10.95

INNER CIRCLE by Claire McNab. 208 pp. 8th Carol Ashton
Mystery.   ISBN 1-56280-135-X   10.95

LESBIAN SEX: AN ORAL HISTORY by Susan Johnson.
240 pp. Need we say more?   ISBN 1-56280-142-2   14.95

BABY, IT'S COLD by Jaye Maiman. 256 pp. 5th Robin Miller
Mystery.   ISBN 1-56280-141-4   19.95

WILD THINGS by Karin Kallmaker. 240 pp. By the undisputed
mistress of lesbian romance.   ISBN 1-56280-139-2   10.95

THE GIRL NEXT DOOR by Mindy Kaplan. 208 pp. Just what
you'd expect.   ISBN 1-56280-140-6   10.95

NOW AND THEN by Penny Hayes. 240 pp. Romance on the
westward journey.   ISBN 1-56280-121-X   10.95

HEART ON FIRE by Diana Simmonds. 176 pp. The romantic and
erotic rival of *Curious Wine*.   ISBN 1-56280-152-X   10.95

DEATH AT LAVENDER BAY by Lauren Wright Douglas. 208 pp.
1st Allison O'Neil Mystery.   ISBN 1-56280-085-X   10.95

YES I SAID YES I WILL by Judith McDaniel. 272 pp. Hot
romance by famous author.   ISBN 1-56280-138-4   10.95

FORBIDDEN FIRES by Margaret C. Anderson. Edited by Mathilda
Hills. 176 pp. Famous author's "unpublished" Lesbian romance.
                                                ISBN 1-56280-123-6   21.95

SIDE TRACKS by Teresa Stores. 160 pp. Gender-bending
Lesbians on the road.   ISBN 1-56280-122-8   10.95

HOODED MURDER by Annette Van Dyke. 176 pp. 1st Jessie
Batelle Mystery.   ISBN 1-56280-134-1   10.95

WILDWOOD FLOWERS by Julia Watts. 208 pp. Hilarious and
heart-warming tale of true love.   ISBN 1-56280-127-9   10.95

NEVER SAY NEVER by Linda Hill. 224 pp. Rule #1: Never get involved
with . . .   ISBN 1-56280-126-0   10.95

THE SEARCH by Melanie McAllester. 240 pp. Exciting top cop
Tenny Mendoza case.   ISBN 1-56280-150-3   10.95

THE WISH LIST by Saxon Bennett. 192 pp. Romance through
the years.   ISBN 1-56280-125-2   10.95

FIRST IMPRESSIONS by Kate Calloway. 208 pp. P.I. Cassidy
James' first case.   ISBN 1-56280-133-3   10.95

OUT OF THE NIGHT by Kris Bruyer. 192 pp. Spine-tingling
thriller.   ISBN 1-56280-120-1   10.95

NORTHERN BLUE by Tracey Richardson. 224 pp. Police recruits
Miki & Miranda — passion in the line of fire. ISBN 1-56280-118-X   10.95

LOVE'S HARVEST by Peggy J. Herring. 176 pp. by the author of
Once More With Feeling.   ISBN 1-56280-117-1   10.95

THE COLOR OF WINTER by Lisa Shapiro. 208 pp. Romantic
love beyond your wildest dreams.   ISBN 1-56280-116-3   10.95

FAMILY SECRETS by Laura DeHart Young. 208 pp. Enthralling
romance and suspense.   ISBN 1-56280-119-8   10.95

INLAND PASSAGE by Jane Rule. 288 pp. Tales exploring conven-
tional & unconventional relationships.   ISBN 0-930044-56-8   10.95

DOUBLE BLUFF by Claire McNab. 208 pp. 7th Carol Ashton
Mystery.   ISBN 1-56280-096-5   10.95

BAR GIRLS by Lauran Hoffman. 176 pp. See the movie, read
the book!   ISBN 1-56280-115-5   10.95

THE FIRST TIME EVER edited by Barbara Grier & Christine
Cassidy. 272 pp. Love stories by Naiad Press authors.
                                          ISBN 1-56280-086-8   14.95

MISS PETTIBONE AND MISS McGRAW by Brenda Weathers.
208 pp. A charming ghostly love story.   ISBN 1-56280-151-1   10.95

CHANGES by Jackie Calhoun. 208 pp. Involved romance and
relationships.   ISBN 1-56280-083-3   10.95

These are just a few of the many Naiad Press titles — we are the oldest and
largest lesbian/feminist publishing company in the world. We also offer an
enormous selection of lesbian video products. Please request a complete
catalog. We offer personal service; we encourage and welcome direct mail
orders from individuals who have limited access to bookstores carrying our
publications.